TRAIN STATION
BRIDE

HOLLY BUSH

Chapter One

Boston, 1887

EALLY, JULIA, DO HURRY," JANE Crawford said to her daughter still seated at the ivory lace-covered vanity. "The guests are arriving, and you should be there to greet them."

Julia Crawford smiled up at her mother with resignation. This was a battle she did not need to win. She would make no argument.

"I'll be down shortly, Mother. Jolene and Jennifer are there. Our guests are here to see them, not me. Has Jillian gone down?"

"She is standing with your father at the door," her mother replied.

"I'll be down in a moment, then. Do go down to the guests. You know how father fusses when you leave him alone," Julia said as she spun a blonde curl around her finger.

Her mother glided to the door and closed it softly. Julia cocked her ear, waiting for the soft patter of her mother's slippers on the steps. Only then did she pull the gold chain from her neck and insert the key that hung from it in a gilded jewel box. With a final glance at her bedroom door, Julia pulled a white envelope from the case and unfolded the letter it held.

Dear Miss Crawford,

I will be at the train station to meet you on the appointed day. My mother and I look forward to your arrival. I will stay above my shop until the day of our marriage. My mother has graciously allowed you to stay with her during that time. She is pleased to know you do needlepoint. Her arthritic hands no longer allow her to sew, and she is most anxious to have another woman about. I am anxious as well . . .

Julia read to the last line even though she could have recited the letter as if it were the Lord's Prayer. *Very truly, Mr. Jacob Snelling.* The day would arrive for her to depart sooner than she both hoped and dreaded. Mr. Snelling was a successful shop owner, near fifty years old, with an aging mother in a small South Dakota town. He had never married. His mother had begun to complain of a lack of company, and he admitted he was lonely. Those two forces had led him to place an ad for a wife in the Boston Globe nearly a year ago. And to Julia's shock she had answered it. Their correspondence had been proper, more formal than she had expected from a merchant in the Midwest.

That formality had been a great comfort to her. It was what she was accustomed to. And he sounded like a truly nice man. He had great regard for his mother, of that Julia was certain. His letters were filled with news of the aging Portentia Snelling and that always brought comfort to Julia when she was most terrified of what she was embarking on. A man so devoted to his own mother would certainly be kind to her. Julia rose from the vanity seat with a smile on her face. One more formal evening with her family could not deter her now.

Julia was not sure of the sentiment only a few minutes later. She greeted a few guests and found an unoccupied chair in the corner of the library. She had spent much of the day arranging the fresh flowers that now filled the room. It had kept her mind and hands occupied while her sisters fussed over their wardrobe and their mother had scolded the servants over some small matter. Without distractions, the day would have dragged on, and she would have dwelled on a decision her mind had yet to grasp. Julia gazed absently about the room.

Her older sister, Jolene, married now ten years with a beautiful, fair child, sashayed about on the arm of her husband, Turner Crenshaw. Julia's younger sister, Jennifer, nearly twenty-one, sat amidst a bevy of Boston's first sons, laughing sweetly and tilting her head just so. It was most certainly the sin of envy that would lead her straight to Hades in the afterlife.

Julia felt no jealousy, though, as her eyes found Jillian. The baby of the family. Jillian would spend the first hour of the party with the adults and then be whisked away to her rooms. Only ten-years-old and already beautiful enough to turn male heads. Dressed in navy velvet with a cream-colored lace collar to match her hair, Julia was certain Jillian was the fairest of the Crawford family. Even at her young age she was a model of deportment and graciousness with a gay laugh and shining blonde hair. Julia would miss her most of all.

The Crawford women were all tall and slender except Julia. She was no higher than her father's tiepin at fourteen and still exactly the same height at twenty-seven. Julia snatched three shrimp from the young serving girl's tray as she passed and laid them beside four chocolate bon-bons in the napkin on her lap. Julia preferred to refer to herself as pleasingly plump, or on the days before her monthly courses, as a fat, frothy, ugly spinster with perfectly beautiful siblings and parents.

Julia was licking chocolate from her fingers when she saw her mother staring. Jane Crawford excused herself from her guests gracefully, as she did everything in life,

Julia had long ago decided. Gracefully floating, serene and above the clutter and clamor of normal living. She had attempted to instill that elegance to each of her children. Julia was certain her mother considered her second daughter her greatest failure.

"Julia, use a napkin," Jane chided and turned her head to view the crowd in their formal sitting room. "Alred McClintok has been hoping to speak to you all evening. Why don't you quit hiding in this corner and go talk to him?"

Julia dabbed chocolate from the corner of her mouth and looked at the man her mother was referring to. Did everyone assume that plump women were only attracted to fat men? One of the reasons Julia continued writing Mr. Snelling was because of his description of himself early on in their writing. *I am of medium height and very thin. Dear Mama worries I am ill, but Dr. Hammish assures me . . .* Alred McClintok was busy stuffing canapés in his mouth, leaving a trail of grease around his fleshy red lips. He reminded Julia of a large black ball propped on two very stubby sticks.

"I'm perfectly happy here, Mother. Your party seems a rousing success," Julia said. Changing subjects had been a tact Julia had used successfully when conversation turned her direction, especially with her father and Jennifer. Her mother and Jolene, however, rarely allowed such a diversion unless it was to their advantage.

Julia knew she had failed when her mother gave her a glare she was long accustomed to. The icy blue of her mother's eyes and the pinched shell of her mouth screamed spinster, on the shelf, and a long list of other shortcomings without saying a word.

"Mr. McClintok is an associate of your father's, dear. We must always endeavor to make your father's business prosperous. Household expenses only seem to rise, rather than fall," her mother said.

The veiled reference to Julia's dependence on her parent's home did not escape her. She also knew her family's business was very successful. Feeding and clothing her would never send them to the poor house. Julia glanced at the shrimp still lying in the napkin on her lap. Maybe she'd best go speak to the man. Nothing would come of a quick introduction and might keep her from expanding her waistline yet another inch. If he spit lamb on her gown, she could go to her rooms to change and not emerge until morning. Or she would slip to her room via the servant's staircase in the kitchen and check her bags already packed and stacked in the dressing room of her bedroom. On the morrow there would be only three days until she departed.

Julia had hoarded every bit of silver she could for her trip. The letter to her family was written, as well as a separate one for Jillian. Their maid, Eustace, would give them out when she didn't arrive home from a weeklong visit with Aunt Mildred. By that time she would be married, and there would be nothing her family could do.

Jolene would roll her eyes. Jennifer would be sad. Not for long, though. Her father would rant and rave. Her mother's fury would be hidden behind a glassy stare. Though, all in all, Julia was sure they would be glad she was gone. They would never voice the sentiment, for certain. Would be gauche to admit this final lapse in judgment would, thankfully, be the last, in their company at the least. They would tell friends Julia was on an extended holiday at Aunt Mildred's. Just as they had done before. Soon no one would inquire as to when she would be coming home. Her family least of all.

The only person other than their housekeeper, Eustace, who would miss her would be Jillian. No more long walks in the park. No more reading together by candlelight with the rest of the household long abed. No more brushing the girls' silken hair till the child's eyes drooped. Jane Crawford supposed Jillian preferred Julia's company because Julia often acted with the sense of a ten-year-old rather than a woman. Julia would insist that Jillian loved the freedom to just be herself in Julia's company. For whichever reason, they would miss each other desperately.

But it was long past time that Julia did something for herself. Make something of herself. Even if it was to only be a wife to a thin, balding Midwesterner and a companion for his mother. She could have lived indefinitely with Aunt Mildred. Her aunt had written her as much. Julia loved the woman and her aunt adored her, but Mildred at seventy-two had an active life with other widowers in the seaside town she lived in. And a beau in his eighty-fourth year. As Mrs. Jacob Snelling, she was someone of her own making. Someone's wife. Something no one could take away from her.

Awakened from her daydreaming, Julia realized her mother had drifted on. She let out a sigh of relief and rose from her chair, having made her obligatory appearance and feeling quite content to reread Mr. Snellings's letter until she fell asleep. Her escape to the kitchens was thwarted by Jolene.

"Julia, come here," her elder sister said hurriedly. When Julia was within arms reach, Jolene pulled her close. "I do believe Mr. McClintok would love to talk to you. Stay right here with Turner, and I'll fetch him."

Before Julia could form a reply, Jolene was off in a whirl of pale blue silk. Julia looked at her brother-in-law from the corner of her eye. "Hello, Turner."

"Ah, how are you, Julia?" Turner asked.

Turner Crenshaw was strikingly handsome. And rich. He and Jolene made a very attractive couple, much in demand at social functions. Jolene's throaty laugh and elegance combined with Turner's good looks and business success made them *the* couple to emulate. Turner was always comfortable and in command, other than when he was forced to converse with his wife's rather eccentric and spinster sister.

"I'm fine, Turner. Thank you for asking. How is William?" Julia asked.

"Quite the little man, already," Turner replied with a smile.

The ensuing silence stretched on. As usual they had little to say to one another. Julia never pictured Turner as the brother she never had. Exactly the opposite, in fact. There was nothing sisterly about how her heart raced when Turner's face broke into a beautiful smile. This was the most compelling reason to board that westbound train. She wasn't eccentric. She was pitiful. Pining after her sister's husband, year after year.

"William is so handsome already. He'll break hearts all over Boston, I fear," she said.

Turner agreed with a nod and gazed over the crowd, stopping as his wife leaned her head back to laugh. "With a mother as lovely as Jolene, I had little fear our children would not be beautiful." Turner tilted his head and stared at his wife with passion and reverence. "She is the perfect mother, the perfect hostess. I am indeed a lucky man."

Julia swallowed and turned to him with a shaky smile. "My sister is accomplished. The essence of all my mother's work. But Jolene is lucky as well."

Turner's face reddened slowly from his neck to his ears. "Julia, I did not mean to go on so about her."

Jolene arrived with her prize in tow. "Julia, darling. Have you been introduced to Mr. McClintok?" Jolene said as she clutched Julia's arm. "I know you would just love to meet him."

Jolene *loved* everything. Her new hat. Her son. Crisp stationary. Hard working servants. Her husband. Julia didn't understood how Jolene bandied about a word such as love without an ounce of insight to its meaning.

"A pleasure, Mr. McClintok," Julia said.

Alred McClintok shifted his plate overflowing with teacakes to the hand already holding a crystal champagne glass. "Miss Crawford," he said with a meaty smile.

"Alred here is making quite a name for himself at Federal Bank. Up and coming, you know," Turner said and winked at Julia. "I hear his home on Monfort Street has fourteen bedrooms."

Julia smiled wanly as the rotund man rubbed his tongue over his gums. Turner and Jolene's measure of success was money and what it bought. They always introduced people with a clear indication of their status in the financial world. As if she cared one fig that the piggish man had seven hundred bedrooms. She would never be in any of them.

"I hear your stables are extraordinary," Jolene added for good measure.

The fat man's head bobbed. "Yes, yes. I've managed to assemble some of the handsomest and most valuable stock in Boston."

The three of them turned to Julia expectantly. As if she should respond, 'Yes, I'll marry you. You have nice horses, and I'm twenty seven, unmarried and a hair over weight.' Julia watched her sister's mouth turn from a beautiful smile to a grim expectant line. She had to say something. Hopefully something as witty and charming as Jolene or Jennifer would.

"You don't say," Julia replied.

Jolene's shoulders dropped, their alabaster skin sinking further into white lace. Turner glanced absently around the room. He had done his duty, Julia supposed. She tried to suppress the embarrassment she felt when Turner was witness to one of these humiliating scenes. Her head snapped up when Alred McClintok belched. He smiled at her and drank the rest of his champagne. Julia's mouth tightened, and she supposed those up-and-coming souls with Turner and Jolene Crenshaw at their sides had no need of good manners.

"A 'pardon me' would do just fine," Julia said.

Alred McClintok sputtered and hurried away as Turner reached for his wife's arm. Jolene faced her sister. "Really, Julia. Is it necessary to be rude?"

"Rude?" Julia asked. "He belched in my face without so much as an 'excuse me'."

Turner took hold of Jolene's elbow as if to guide her away. Jolene glared at her husband. "I believe Father needs you, Turner." Jolene dropped her head for a moment and looked up to present her husband a charming smile. "You do know how he loves to show you off."

Julia watched Turner clip off a nod to his wife. The two sisters stood in silence. Jolene used the same tactics their mother did. Stony, unrelenting silence until the suspected party blubbered out all of their transgressions.

"Say your peace, Jolene," Julia finally said when the quiet was eventually overwhelming.

Jolene nodded to a passing guest and turned a cold face her sister's way. "Is it absolutely necessary for you to chase off every possible suitor? Is it your grand design to be an . . . .an . . ."

"An embarrassment? Jolene, I have humiliated this family in more grandiose ways than the simple observance of an appalling lack of manners," Julia said.

"Have you no pride left, Julia? Do you wish to live in your parents' home until your doderage? Don't you want a home of your own? A husband?"

Tears clung stubbornly to Julia's lashes. She whispered for fear of screaming her reply. "Yes, no and yes. I had dreams too, Jolene. Dreams of a handsome man and a home of my own. My dreams died with one glance at my older, thin, tall, beautiful sister. And because I have pride left, I have no intention of marrying the only man left in Boston who would take to bride a short, fat spinster with well-heeled relatives."

"You are attractive in your own way, Julia. You are not thin, granted, but certainly not the fat round spinster you make yourself out to be. And the only reason Mother and I keep introducing you to eligible men is because we want you to be happy. Have a home and children of your own."

"I have a home, Jolene." The subject of children was more than Julia could possible speak about without tears and hysterias. "I have given up everything for the good of this family. I will not sacrifice my self-respect."

Jolene's cheeks tightened. She stretched her arm out to a guest and glided along with a smile to greet them.

* * *

The stars shown brightly as Julia lay in her bed and stared out the window. The last guests had finally left, and Julia could hear tidbits of conversation from the foyer. Jolene, Jennifer and her mother were reviewing the evening. Delicious food. The right people. Jennifer's way with the bachelors. Turner and Jolene's invitation to the governor's mansion. A smashing success. Then a prolonged silence. "Rude to Mr. McClintok?" "Oh dear." "What's to be done?" Heavy, thoughtful sighs followed.

As if she was nine-years-old again and spilled a glass of milk on her mother's Belgian lace tablecloth while the mayor and his wife dined with them. Or when she tore the hem of her Christmas dress just as the family alighted from the carriage in front of the church steps and all of Boston's good society. Or when at fourteen she slapped the son of her father's business partner for kissing her. He told everyone she had been trying to kiss him, and the mark on his face was left when he tried to avoid her lips and bumped into the doorjamb. The shattering of a priceless vase had been her fault as well.

Julia pulled the coverlet over herself and rolled onto her side. Soon the plague of the Crawford family would be one thousand miles away. And maybe, just maybe, Julia thought, she would find a peaceful, useful existence away from censure and judgment, without constant reminders of her failures. South Dakota could not have seemed more like the promised land to Julia than heaven itself.

South Dakota 1887

Jake Shelling stood in the doorway of his home and breathed a sigh of relief and happiness as his youngest sister rolled away in the wagon. Gloria was twenty, married a year and expecting her first child in the fall. Her happiness had been the last remaining item on his mental list, finally clearing a path for his own plans since his sisters' upbringing had fallen to him when their parents had both died of influenza. Jake could still picture himself at the ripe old age of sixteen holding his sisters' hands as men lowered their mother and father's caskets into the bleak South Dakota prairie.

Flossie was nine the day they had died and Gloria a mere three-years-old. The first five years from that day had been the hardest he would have sworn at the time. A barely cleared farm, a half-built house and no relatives nearby to help. Years later he would have said the worst time was when Flossie went to her first dance and Gloria's husband Will had begun hanging around.

Jake had made it through his sister's suitors, blizzards and a rocky start to where he found himself now. Thirty-three years old and just beginning to think about what he wanted to do for himself. The land had fulfilled just as his father had promised and had provided money in the bank, as well as dowries for his sisters.

Jake turned down the hallway of his two-story farmhouse and headed for the kitchen. No rug padded his feet, and no pictures or heirlooms hung on the walls. The sitting room he passed held two horsehair chairs in front of an unlit fireplace. Doo-dads weren't necessary; he told Flossie when she scolded him about the state of their parent's home. His sister was always trying to brighten things up with curtains and pictures, but Jake wanted none of it. His now deadly quiet house was where he slept and ate. He didn't need throw pillows to accomplish that.

But he had decided what it did need. A woman. He supposed he would let her fuss a bit if she had to, buying fabric and gewgaws. But they weren't going to get in the way of his plan. A woman to cook and mend and a son to pass his years of sacrifice and work on to. His sisters' husbands had farms of their own, and when Jake let himself wallow, he imagined his own burial with his nieces and nephews standing at the graveside wondering what to do with the barren house and farm of their uncle's other than to sell it to a stranger.

Jake Shelling had no intention of letting his parent's graves and legacy fall into the hands of a buyer that was not of his parent's stock. He would have a son, regular meals, sex without buying it and someone to work the farm towards a common goal. Yep, marriage was going to suit him just fine, Jake thought as he poured himself a cup of lukewarm coffee. This time.

Shortly after Gloria's wedding last spring he had arranged to marry a woman, a cousin of his closest neighbor. Valerie Morton had been reported to be an attractive, hard-working woman ready to tie the knot. He had let himself hope to find some of the happiness his sisters had with their husbands. Not love necessarily but comfort and companionship. It was not meant to be. Valerie Morton had married the owner of the Brass Jug Saloon on her trip to be Jake's bride.

So much for the exchanged letters and promises. He'd been embarrassed to realize he'd never given a thought to the possibility that his intended would not hold true to her word. The day he received her letter saying she would marry him, he'd considered her part of his family. Valerie Morton didn't honor commitments the same way he and his sisters always had. He had misplaced his trust and been sorely disappointed.

But this time, he had planned better. Jake ordered a bride from Sweden of all places he thought to himself and chuckled. A young widow with no children, wanting to make America her home. He supposed he could live with not being able to understand what his wife was saying as long as she was as strong and reliable as the agency in New York reported. So he had sent three hundred dollars four months ago and his bride, all six foot of her, was to arrive tomorrow. A tall woman wouldn't bother him, he imagined. She wouldn't be taller than him after all.

Flossie and Gloria had scolded him something awful, and his brothers-in-law, Will and Harry, had laughed till they cried when Jake told them of his plans. He told Pastor Phillips to meet him at the station at three o'clock on Friday. He was going to marry Inga Crawper at the railway platform before the B & O chugged away. And he was hoping and praying Miss Crawper's eight brothers were proof of a good chance of having sons. He didn't want daughters, that he knew for certain. Jake didn't think he would live through someone courting his child. It had been hard enough with Gloria and Flossie. Yep, things were going to work out just fine.

Chapter Two

"T HERE IS NO NEED FOR you to come to the train station, Mother," Julia said.

Her last few days in her parents' home had crept by. Finally it was time to begin the plan Julia had put into motion so many months ago. But now, her palms were sweating and her heart racing, and it wasn't entirely due to riding a train for three days and marrying a man she had never met. Jane Crawford had announced she would ride to the station with Julia and have Tom, their stable man, take her to town for some shopping on the same trip. Eustace stood in the doorway of the morning room. If Jane Crawford went to the train station, she would know Julia's ticket was for South Dakota, not Delaware bound for Aunt Mildred's.

"Mrs. Crawford. I . . . I've lost the menus we went over yesterday. I'm sorry but Cook needs to order for the weekend, and I can't remember everything you told me about the dinner party on Monday," Eustace said.

"Really, Eustace. How clumsy of you. Where did you put the list?" Jane Crawford asked.

"I've looked everywhere for it, Ma'am. I just can't find it," Eustace replied.

Jane Crawford's face was pinched and sour, as it always was when any detail of living like an unintentionally misplaced list interfered with her plans. Especially when it involved a servant. Julia knew her mother would make Eustace's life miserable in small ways, and she appreciated the sacrifice. Most likely Jane Crawford would find an excuse to need Eustace on Sunday and keep the woman from visiting her sickly mother.

"I'm sure Eustace didn't lose the list on purpose. Accidents do happen, Mother. Stay here and help her rewrite it, and I'll send Tom back from the station as quickly as I can. You'll be able to shop all afternoon. Maybe Jolene will be done with her committee meeting and go with you," Julia said.

Jane Crawford blew a breath through her tiny nose. "Jolene does need to order new outfits for William. I suppose I can wait. But I do hate for you to stand unattended at the train depot, Julia."

"No one will carry me away at nine o'clock in the morning, Mother," Julia said as she pulled on her lace gloves.

Jane arched her brows but relented. "I suppose not. Although it is unseemly." She straightened her skirts and looked at Julia. "You are packed?"

"Tom has everything in the carriage already. I said goodbye to Jennifer and to . . ." Julia took a deep breath and continued, "and to Jillian. I kissed Father goodbye last night and sent a note off to Jolene." Julia stood and swallowed a lump of fear in her throat. "I'm ready to go."

"Well, fine then, dear," Jane said and tilted her cheek up for a kiss. "Tell your Aunt Mildred we said hello."

Julia walked to her mother slowly, smelling the scent of roses wafting to her as she approached. She knew there were tears in her eyes but could do nothing but keep walking. Julia bent, put her mouth near her mother's ear. "Goodbye, Mother. Take care of . . . of everyone."

Jane Crawford tilted her head and eyed Julia suspiciously. "You're only going for a week, Julia. No need to get emotional. I'll have Tom at the station next Friday."

Julia smiled and nodded. "Of course, Mother. I'll see you very soon then."

Julia walked from the sitting room and hugged Eustace tightly where the woman stood waiting anxiously in the hallway. She could smell the starch in Eustace's black uniform.

"Thank you, Eustace, for everything," she whispered.

Eustace choked back a sob. "Everything's going to work out for you, girl. You just wait and see."

"I love you," Julia said. Eustace nodded, and Julia pulled away without looking at the face she had come to treasure. Julia hurried down the hallway and didn't stop till old Tom had her safely seated in the carriage. The last thing she heard as she exited her home of twenty-seven years was Eustace's compliance to Jane Crawford's insistence that all of the silver in the household would need polished Sunday afternoon. The last thing she saw from the carriage window was Jillian's face pressed tightly to the glass of the second story bedroom window as the child waved goodbye.

* * *

Friday arrived clear and warm, and Jake went to the bunkhouse to tell Slim he was leaving for the day. They reviewed what was to be done while one of the hands hitched the wagon. Just as Jake thought he'd made a clear get away, he saw Flossie riding into the yard. Jake stood beside the wagon till she rode up close. She slapped her hat on her leg, releasing a cloud of dust and slid down the side of her horse in one smooth motion.

"You're going through with this crazy plan of yours, aren't you?" Flossie said.

"Where's the kids?" Jake replied.

"Don't you go changing the subject on me, Jake Shelling. You can't fool me. Never could."

Jake tilted his hat back and sat his hands on his hips. He looked out on the horizon. "What do you want me to do, Floss? I'm not getting any younger."

"I've tried to introduce you to some nice women, Jake. You never even call on them," she replied.

"I don't have time to go wandering all over the countryside, carrying flowers and picking up hankies. I need a wife and a son. And a decent cook if I'm lucky. I don't need a love match like Gloria and Will."

"Like Gloria and Will?" Flossie asked.

"You know what I mean, Floss. Harry suits you and you suit him, but he didn't stand around mooney-eyed reading poetry. You needed a husband, Harry needed a wife, and you two seem to do just fine."

Flossie barked a laugh. "You still don't know, do you?"

"Know what?" Jake asked.

"Harry and I did plenty of courting, including more than just kissing right there behind that barn," Flossie said and pointed. "Even some poetry and flowers. Just because Harry and I don't hang all over each other in public like Gloria and Will doesn't mean there isn't something special about what we do with each other and for each other in private."

Jake looked away and made a face like he had just eaten a bite of green apple. "Jeez, Flossie, don't tell me this stuff."

"I'm not talking about the marriage bed," Flossie said. "I'm talking about love. Cripes sakes, anyway, Jake, you were the one that told me about getting my monthly courses. Did you think we had Danny and Millie without going to bed together?"

"I try not to think about it, Floss."

Flossie shook her head. "Here you've gone and changed the subject. The problem is you're going to the train station dragging the minister to marry a woman you've never even seen. You don't know anything about her."

"I knew plenty about Valerie Morton. That didn't get me a bride," Jake responded with a grim smile.

"Oh, for Pete's sakes. When are you going to get it that not all woman are lying, pieces of uppity fluff like Miss Valerie Morton?" Flossie shouted.

"I don't know if I ever will, Floss. I put a lot of thinking and planning into that woman, and it didn't work out. I don't want to do it again. The agency in New York guaranteed me Inga Crawper would arrive at the station unwed."

Flossie closed the distance between herself and her brother. "I know you don't want to be disappointed. I don't want you to. You spent your whole life making sure Gloria and I had everything we needed and didn't spend much time on yourself. But that doesn't mean you won't meet a woman you could love. That would make you happy. I want you to be happy, Jake."

"If you want me to be happy, let me get to the train station on time, Flossie. This is what I want," Jake replied.

"Harry and I and the kids will be over about six o'clock. Gloria and Will, too. If this is what you want, we intend to welcome this Inga to the family the right way. Even if she won't understand a damn word we say."

Jake kissed Flossie on the cheek. "I imagine you'll make her understand. You've never had too much trouble getting your point across. I can't see a little problem like a foreign language stopping you. Now get on home before Harry sees you riding alone. You got your six-shooter, don't you?"

Flossie climbed in the saddle, blew a kiss to Jake and turned her horse towards home. "I'll be careful. Harry knows where I was going. I left him in the barn holding Millie, hollering his head off. I imagine he'll be about done screaming by the time I get home."

* * *

Jake was whistling a tune by the time he pulled into town. It was a glorious day, he was going to be married and his sister had come to terms with his decision. If Flossie accepted Inga, then the rest of the family would follow suit. That was a load off Jake's mind. Nothing, not this marriage, nor the land or his parent's graves were as important to Jake as family. He would have died before letting anything happen to Flossie or Gloria and Millie and Danny. He imagined that sentiment extended to Harry and Will as well. And he knew Gloria and Flossie felt the same way. They would make Inga's transition smooth and would learn to love her even if he didn't. It was how his family worked. The result of three children left alone to defend and feed themselves on the prairie. Through tornadoes, hunger and grief they had never deserted each other.

Chapter Three

J ULIA'S TRAIN TRIP WAS DIRTY and hot. But she did enjoy looking out the window at the changing scenery and tried not to dwell on what she had left behind. She would arrive in a few hours in the town of Cedar Ridge.

Early that morning she had carried her valise to the water closet. She had rinsed her mouth and changed her dress and underclothes in the small room. It had been a battle nearly lost in the tiny, bouncing cupboard. But she was seated now and cooled down in the breeze in a pale yellow, cinched waist organdy dress. Julia had repined her hair and settled a matching yellow hat with chin-length netting that covered her whole face. For the trip she had forgone the heavy boning under her traveling suit, but this morning had managed to get a full set of petticoats, corsets and stays in the right place. Julia certainly didn't want Mr. Snelling to meet her dressed in less than the proper way. She needed to make a good impression. There would be no going back.

Jane Crawford would be proud, Julia thought with a wry smile. I will manage to arrive in a prairie town looking every inch the proper Boston lady. Matching hat, gloves and reticule. A fitted, fashionable gown that showed off her pale coloring to the best effect. She had managed to hold back tears most of the trip. As the conductor called out Cedar Ridge, she did not know if she could any longer. She refused to admit to herself she was scared to death. Petrified. Of a new town far away from everyone and everything she ever knew. A man. A marriage. All the things she was sure she wanted.

Julia forced a smile to her face and imagined meeting her future husband for the first time. If she held her purse strings tight enough, Mr. Snelling would never see how badly her hands shook. If she pulled the yellow netting down over her chin, demurely, he would never see her lips tremble and the terror in her eyes. She would nod and speak little so he did not hear the tremor in her voice. She would meet his mother and settle into the small house with her. Maybe Mr. Snelling would take her to dinner tonight. Begin to get to know each other before their wedding next Saturday. Dear Lord, she thought, I'll be married next Saturday.

The train began to slow down, and Julia could see from the window a huge crowd of people milling about.

Banners were hung, and she thought she could hear the blare of an Oompah band. It looked as though the train tracks ran right through the middle of a town that sprawled out in all directions and was larger than she had expected. Her mouth was dry and her nerves shakier with each slowing chug of the train and each passing street sign. Finally the locomotive stopped with a loud steamed belch, and other passengers stood up in the aisle. Julia rose, took a deep breath and wondered what had ever prompted her to reply to Mr. Snelling's ad.

Julia stood on the step of the train and looked at the vast crowd of people. Her departure from her lifetime home was the least of her problems at this moment. How would she ever find Mr. Snelling in this crush?

The conductor shouted in her ear that her trunks and bags were being deposited on the boardwalk, one car down. Julia thanked him and hurried to find her things. It was difficult, working her way through the throng especially being at best shoulder height with some of the shorter men and women. She found her leather strapped trunk and her other bags and planted herself beside them, looking through the mob for a fiftyish, balding, thin man. It was impossible. She couldn't see further than a lapel. She stood on tiptoe with no better results. Julia had to get a better view but didn't want to leave her luggage to find a higher vantage point.

Julia stared down at her trunk. Glory hallelujah. Her trunk. She would stand on it and have a clear view of all the faces milling about. Her mother and Jolene would have a fit if they knew what she was thinking of doing. Better though to imagine their censure than find herself east bound if she couldn't find Mr. Snelling. She had no doubt her father would be sending someone to escort her home. Julia had to be married when that day arrived.

* * *

Jake inched his way through the crowd, Pastor Phillips in tow. He had forgotten completely about the Founder's Day Celebration. Town was packed with every farmer, rancher and their families for miles around. He wondered if Flossie was keeping her family home because of his new bride coming to town. If so, Danny and Millie would have a thing or two to say to their Uncle Jake about missing the biggest party of the year. He didn't need to crane his neck much to look for his bride-to-be. He towered over most of the crowd. And he figured Miss Crawper would be easy to spot. A woman near six foot tall. He guessed she'd be blonde. Hadn't he read somewhere that most folks from those Norwegian countries were blonde? Jake straightened up as he saw upswept blonde hair under a yellow hat. He grabbed the Pastor's arm and yanked him through the crowd.

"Miss Crawper," he shouted when he finally got close enough. "I'm Jake Shelling." The train shifted on the track as the woman turned. Jake couldn't hear her reply but he could see the gauzy fabric moving in front of her mouth.

Miss Crawper sure was gussied up in fancy clothes for a widow woman just off the boat. Jake didn't know much about fashions but having listened to his two sisters for as many years as he had made him sure this woman was wearing expensive, fashionable clothing. He introduced Pastor Phillips over the roar of the crowd. The woman seemed to stand in a daze. But then Jake realized she had no idea what he was talking about.

"And you're sure you want to do this, Miss Crawper?" Pastor Phillips shouted.

The woman's head turned from the Pastor and back to Jake. The crowd shouted in unison as the woman replied, and he was being elbowed and bumped by every man jack that went by. Jake was pretty sure she had repeated her name.

"We know who you are," Jake said slowly and very loud as if he were talking to a child. He pointed to his chest, then to her, then to the bible held in the minister's hand. He motioned as if putting a ring on his finger. She nodded.

Pastor Phillips took the woman's hand, placed it in Jakes' and opened his book. She looked up at him and then at the pastor. He couldn't see her face clearly, but he could tell she was a beautiful woman. He had expected her to be big-boned. But for her near six foot, this woman was dainty. Not skinny with no meat on her bones but round, and soft and sweet smelling. Delicate looking and shiny as the intricate yellow fabric she wore.

Just glowing like the sun from the top of her yellow hat to the matching purse.

The pastor elbowed Jake as he closed his book. Jake slipped the ring over white gloves . . . and hell's fire. His bride had fainted. Jake caught her in his arms as the crowd began to thin away to watch the rodeo scheduled in the pasture behind the train station. Pastor Phillips was fanning her with his hat. Jake held his new bride in his arms easily and surveyed her from her head to her yellow shoes. Hell, this woman wasn't six foot tall. She wasn't five foot tall. Jake looked down at the station platform beside him. A black trunk sat there. Good God. She'd been standing on a trunk. This couldn't be Inga Crawper. Who in the hell had he just married?

* * *

Julia woke up slowly as the air around her cooled. At first she hadn't the foggiest notion where she was. Then she thought she was having her favorite dream. Waking up in the arms of a handsome man. But she wasn't in her bedroom in Boston. She was in South Dakota.

Everything tumbled back in to her mind. The dreadful shouting and noise that had kept her from hearing her own wedding words were now distant. Her wonder as to why Mr. Snelling had changed his plans, marrying her here and now and not waiting a week as he had written her. Her shock when she got her first look at her husband to be. He would have been a giant had she not been standing on her trunk. The train had pulled away, and the platform where her trunks sat was near empty.

Julia was too petrified too move. Her husband wore a hat so she could did see his balding head. He was much more handsome than she'd expected. And big. How could have his own mother worried he were too thin? He looked as though he could lift the train from the tracks had he wanted. He wasn't fat but he was nothing like the spindly, shy man she had envisioned. And to her gross mortification she had fainted in his arms.

"Mr. Snelling?" she asked.

"It's Jake Shelling. Who the hell are you?" he replied.

"Mr. Snelling, you mean. Mr. Jacob Snelling. My fiancé. Why I'm your bride," Julia said. He was staring down at her and then turned with a monstrous look to the minister.

"Give me that license, Pastor," he said.

The man in black pursed his lips and shook his head. "Nope. I married ya right and proper, Jake. This here's your bride. For better or worse."

Julia turned her head and he did as well when they heard shouting from the train depot house. "Miss Crawford. Miss Julia Crawford?"

Julia fluttered her hands against his chest. "Please put me down. Someone's calling my name."

"Julia Crawford," he said.

"Yes," she replied as her husband lowered her to the wooden platform. She lifted her hand in a wave. "I'm

Julia Crawford. I mean, I was, I mean . . ." A thin, balding man was hurrying to her. Julia looked at her giant of a husband and back to the man calling her name frantically. When she saw an aging woman trailing behind the man, recognition occurred.

"Mr. Snelling," she whispered. As the man came towards her motioning the older woman along she realized he was the man she was to have married. Julia looked up to the man beside her and back to the thin man holding his hat and calling her name.

"Oh, dear," she said.

The giant blew out a breath. "We got a problem, Snelling."

"What problem, Jake? Other than you seem to be standing awful close to my fiancé," Mr. Snelling said. He smiled wistfully. "I'd recognize her anywhere."

"Jake here's right, Jacob. There's a problem. You see I already married this woman to Jake," Pastor Phillips said.

Jacob Snelling's smile dropped as his hat fell out of his hand.

The old woman peered around her son's shoulder. "I told you, Jacob. You can't trust those city women. Married the first man she saw when she got off the train."

Julia had no idea what to say. The old woman was right. She looked up at her husband. "What did you say your name was, sir?"

"Jake Shelling."

Julia turned to the minister. "There's been a mistake. The names are similar and over the crowd noise, I thought he said his name was Snelling. Mr. Jacob Snelling. You'll have to void or do whatever you must. I was to marry this gentleman here," Julia said and looked at the forlorn man standing in front of her.

"Only way to undo a marriage, Ma'am, is death or divorce. You can file down at the courthouse. Might take a year or so to get, though," he said.

"A divorce," the old woman shouted. "No son of mine is marrying used goods. Snelling's don't marry divorcees."

"But, Mrs. Snelling, I had no idea I was marrying the wrong man," Julia cried.

Jacob Snelling looked at his mother. "I don't know, Mother. It wasn't her fault." He looked back at Julia. "But a divorcee?"

The whole of the assemblage turned when the sheriff escorted a tall blonde woman with long braided ponytails to them. She curtsied and said, "Inga Crawper. Husband. Jake Shelling."

The minister scratched his head. "I'll be betting this here's your foreign bride."

"Hey, Jake. This woman's looking for you. I think she's planning to marry you. Ain't that something?" the sheriff said.

"We've got a problem, Sheriff," Jacob Snelling said. "Jake Shelling stole my bride. Up and married her before I could get here. Mother's feet were bothering her this morning, and I had to rub them with camphor. Made me late. But still all in all, he married the woman I was supposed to."

"She'll be a divorcee, Jacob. We don't want her now," the old woman said.

"Don't suppose somebody could explain this mess to me. And right quick. The mayor's set to make his speech soon, and he wants me up on the platform with him," the man with the tin badge said.

Julia's new husband told the tale and finished with a curse. "And Phillips here won't tear up the license even though there was a mistake. I was to marry Inga Crawper. The one curtseying beside you."

"Scared she was going to get away, Jake?" the sheriff asked.

"Something like that," he replied.

The sheriff rubbed his chin and then his belly. Suddenly his face lit up with a smile.

"Hey, I got it. Snelling, here can marry Inga. It'll all be settled. You both will have a bride. And seeings how you already tied the knot, Jake, you can hardly marry this one, too. Bigamy's illegal in this parts." Sheriff Smith turned to Jacob Snelling. "What do you think, Jacob? Marry Inga here and everything will be solved."

"What do you want?" her new husband asked Julia. "Do you want to file for a divorce so you can marry Jacob Snelling?"

"Used goods, I'm telling you," Mrs. Snelling said, wide-eyed. Her son was staring at the blonde woman from Sweden with a hopeful look on his face.

Julia was humiliated. Her fiancé had barely given her a second glance. His mother stared at her as if she worked in a saloon. The only person who seemed the least bit concerned with her wishes was a man she met ten minutes earlier and had married. And if she filed for divorce, her father would sweep her back to Boston before she could utter a single word of protest. She looked up at him.

"I don't want a divorce," she said.

"Then I guess we're stuck with each other," he said.

Julia stood in the dust of the wooden platform as her new husband turned and stalked away. Inga Crawper was nodding, smiling and bowing to Jacob Snelling. Mrs. Snelling turned to Julia with a smug smile as she latched herself onto the tall blonde's arm to lead her away. The sheriff was already gone, and the minister was having trouble meeting Julia's eyes. Her lips were trembling, and her knees went out from under her. Thankfully, her trunk was behind her. She plopped down with a thud, sending a whirl of dust around her. Julia had no idea what to do. The minister knelt before her, hat in hand.

"Been quite a day, hasn't it?" he asked.

Julia nodded and sniffed.

Pastor Phillips bowed his head and looked up. "I shouldn't be saying this, seeings how Jacob Snelling's a member of my congregation, but I'm thinking the foreigner got the short end of the stick."

Julia looked at him, eyes glistening. "How can you say that? She left with Mr. Snelling and his mother. My husband . . . *my* husband left me here at the station. I don't have any idea what to do, where to go."

"Jake'll be back. Mark my words. No question he's got his hair in an uproar, but Jake Shelling's the most honorable man I know." The Pastor said. "I just think this came as a shock, if you know what I mean."

"A shock? I came here to marry a quiet storekeeper and help care for his mother. I don't know anything about this man. This Jake Shelling. How do you know he'll be back?"

Her circumstances were beginning to sink in. She had read and reread Mr. Snelling's letters so often she felt as if she would be in for few surprises. A twist of fate she could have never envisioned put her into the keeping of a man she knew nothing about.

"Told you. He's honorable. And honest to the core." The Pastor turned his hat in his hand. "You're going have to just trust me on that."

Julia was sure she was in some kind of mental or physical shock. She just did not seem able to make her arms and legs respond to any command. Let alone begin to sort through her thoughts. She saw the pastor rise and turn to look at a wagon approaching. Jake Shelling stopped the horse-driven open wagon up along side the train platform. One long leg stretched from the wagon and he vaulted up beside her. He looked down at her and her things sitting in the heat of the sun.

"All this stuff yours?" he asked.

Julia nodded.

He picked up two cases and heaved them in the wagon. Glass shattered.

"My pictures!" Julia shouted.

"Sorry," he said. He bent down and loaded her trunk on his shoulder.

"Please be careful, sir," Julia said. He turned slowly to face her and frowned. He stepped on to the seat of the rig and put her trunk down carefully behind the seat.

"Better?" he asked.

She looked down at the two remaining bags. "I'll hand these to you."

He accepted the two cases, dropped them beside her trunk and plopped down on the seat. His bride remained standing on the platform. "You coming?" he asked.

Julia swallowed and nodded. The pastor took her hand.

"This is one of those twiny, twirling paths that God puts before us. One step at a time, Mrs. Shelling. One step at a time," Pastor Phillips said.

This strange man, in this new town had called her Mrs. Shelling. Frightening as that thought, the minister's words had given her comfort. The sentiment sounded like something Eustace would have said, and Julia felt tears fill her eyes again. The immediate problem though, the one keeping her from that "twiny, twirling path," was how she was to get in her husband's wagon. She looked up at the pastor.

"I can't decide now whether to be grateful or furious that you won't let us annul this marriage." Julia looked at her hands folded at her waist. "In the mean time do you think you could assist me into the wagon so my husband doesn't desert me?"

Chapter Four

BEFORE THE PASTOR COULD PUT his arm to hers, Jake was out of the wagon standing between her and the minister. He looked from the wagon to the platform to her wide hooped skirt. Flossie would have a fit if he let his new bride fall and break her neck before she got to meet her. Jake lifted his wife in his arms, stepped into the wagon and set her none to cautiously onto the seat. An oomph popped out of her mouth as she tried to straighten her skirts and right her hat. Jake hawed the horse and town and its noise quickly faded to be replaced by complete and utter silence.

"I really couldn't hear you when you said your name," she said.

Jake didn't think the woman had set out to trick him but he was in no mood to make her feel better. He felt too lousy himself. He turned to her. "What is your real name?"

"Julia Crawford. Julia Snelling, I mean Julia Shelling," she stumbled.

Jake whoahed the horses and pulled the break. He faced his wife. "Let's get one thing straight right now. You married me. Not Snelling and his mother. I can't imagine why a woman like you would be batting your lashes for that skinny, mealy-mouthed pain in the ass, but the fact is you married me. Get him out of your head." He took her chin in his hand. "What's mine is mine, and I keep and care for what's mine. Got it?"

"If you're questioning my honor, sir, you needn't. Crawfords keep their word," she said.

Jake eyed her. She was shaking like a leaf in a windstorm, but she spoke her mind anyway. He had to give her credit for that. "Neither do Shellings. And you're a Shelling now. And don't call me 'sir.' I'm Jake. Always have been."

She nodded. "Please call me Julia."

He gave a short snort, released the brake on the wagon and slapped the horses with the reins in his hands. "I intended to."

They rode the distance home without speaking another word. Jake could not believe his second attempt into matrimony had ended like this. He had yet to marry a woman of his choosing. Jake stole a glance at his new bride and couldn't stop himself from wondering what had brought a beautiful woman like her to the prairie of South

Dakota to marry Jacob Snelling and wait on his mother. Jake pulled the wagon up in front of the house.

* * *

Julia stood in the wagon. A brown, weathered house sat a short distance away from a barn and several low flat buildings. Silos rose up from behind. As far as Julia could see lay swaying crops in the fields. The sight was magnificent and terrifying at the same time. Beautiful like a picture Julia had seen in a book and so vast and endless that she felt tiny, insignificant and overwhelmed.

"Does all this land belong to you?" she asked. Her husband had jumped down from the wagon and now was holding out a hand to help her down.

"Does now. Didn't always."

"When did you buy it?" Julia asked.

"My parents bought it in '71. Went to me and my sisters when they died. I gave Flossie her share in cash when she got married. Her and Harry bought a farm just south of here. I gave Gloria a piece of land east of this when she married Will. So what's left is mine. And yours now."

Julia's face paled. There was more information in that clipped speech than she cared to know at this moment. His parents were dead. He had two married sisters who lived nearby. And he was willing to make her part of what was his. Julia didn't want to imagine what his sisters were like. Or their reaction to his marriage. Would they be bossy? Would they point out the fact that she didn't belong here? Didn't have the right to their inheritance? Just as confusing was his acknowledgement of that right. He had said it was hers as well. She turned full around slowly and viewed the land. It was the only solid thing she had ever owned. Julia looked at the ground below her feet. Julia Shelling was a landowner. And her yellow shoes were square on it.

"Come in the house. Out of the sun. Slim'll get your bags," her husband said as she noticed a group of men milling about one of the other buildings.

"That would be nice. It is rather hot."

"You'll have to get used to the heat. And the cold. It's either hot as hell or colder 'en hell," he said and looked down at her dress. "No use wearing all those layers. You'll die of heat exhaustion before the week's out."

Julia gave him a weak smile. He had no idea how appealing it would be to go without a corset and four full petticoats, but then he would notice that her figure was no slim hourglass. She swallowed when it occurred to her he would know eventually. When they went to bed.

Julia walked through her new home. At first she saw little until her eyes adjusted to the dimness. When all was visible, she realized there was little to see. Two chairs in front of a fireplace. No paint or wallpaper on the walls. No pictures. No pillows. No curtains. Absolutely nothing to remind her of her Boston home.

Julia followed Jake into the kitchen and was pleased to see at least this room had the makings of a normal room. A large wooden table with six chairs, a stove and sink. A pie case full of cobwebs. But the sun shone brightly through the windows, and Julia was glad of that. It was at that moment that Julia realized there would probably be no hired help for the house. Mr. Snelling had written that a widowed woman came every morning to clean and prepare dinner. Julia would only have had to serve and do the dishes. Those chores alone seemed at that time a daunting task. She hadn't understood daunting until now.

"Do you employ any inside help, Mr. Shelling?" she asked.

"It's Jake, Julia. We're married. Inside help?" he asked. "You mean like a cleaning woman or a cook?"

She nodded.

"Didn't make much sense to have somebody clean up after me. I've been taking care of things for myself for a long time. I eat at the bunkhouse. Woman from town does come and do the washing once a week," he replied.

Julia slowly sat down on one of the chairs. She looked around the kitchen and knew she had little idea where to begin. "May I have a glass of water?"

He pumped the water into the sink for a while before filling a glass. "My sisters and their families will be here in about an hour. I suppose we ought to know something about each other by then. I'd say things will be a little awkward since they were expecting a six foot tall Swedish woman."

Julia gulped. "Your family's coming to call tonight? In an hour?"

He nodded. "You first."

"Me first?"

"Tell me something about yourself. You're my wife," her husband said.

"But we're getting company. I should change, I should . . ." Julia replied.

"Just family. And your dressed fancier than my sisters will be. Tell me why you came here to marry Snelling."

"Well, Mr. Snelling placed an ad in the Boston Globe for a wife last year. I answered, and we corresponded. He seemed like a kind man in his letters and I agreed to come here and marry him. And help him take care of his mother."

"And?"

"And what?" she asked.

"Come on, Julia. Your family obviously comes from money. Stylish clothes," he said and swept a hand from her head to her toes. "Two trunks full of stuff. Four cases. You're a lady. You're running from something. What is it?"

Julia felt her cheeks redden. "I don't know what you mean." Her lip trembled, and she lowered her lashes.

"If you're running from the law or another husband, I want to know right now," he said.

Julia's mouth dropped. "How dare you. How dare you imply that I'm some sort of fugitive or . . . or runaway."

"Ok, Ok," he said.

"I came here with honest intentions of marrying Mr. Snelling. That's all. And what about you? You could be a murderer for all I know," she said.

"I'm no murderer. Don't imagine Pastor Phillips would have married any woman to a murderer. Tell me about your family."

Certainly he hadn't heard of the Crawford family or her own eccentricities this far west. Julia couldn't imagine what else could concern him. But he was her husband now and she conceded he had some right to know.

"My family? What do you want to know?" Julia asked.

* * *

The whole, long, silent ride home he'd wondered what brought this woman to Cedar Ridge. He didn't want a sheriff or a husband showing up at his door in a month or so. Her denial of any wrongdoing seemed honest enough. But now she was blushing and bowing her head with a simple question about her family. He didn't think the subject was that complicated or should cause a woman to whisper as if she were ashamed.

"Are your parents alive? Do you have brothers and sisters?" he asked.

"William and Jane Crawford are my parents. Their home is in Boston. My sister Jolene is the oldest and married. She and her husband Turner Crenshaw have one child, William. My sister Jennifer is twenty-one. Jillian is ten."

Jake watched intently as she gave far from a warm description of her family. Her face lit up only once when she mentioned the youngest sister. Jillian. An odd wistful look betrayed her when she named her sister's husband.

"All J's, huh?" he said.

"Pardon? Oh yes, all J's. I always thanked God my mother's name was not Zelda," his wife replied.

Jake laughed out loud. It was the first time he had felt like laughing in a long time. And certainly the first time today. "I can understand why." But his bride wasn't laughing. His laugh rolled to a chuckle and then to silence. "Is that all there is to tell?"

"We, excepting myself of course, are a thin attractive family. My father is successful in the shipping industry. My mother and Jolene are perfect hostesses and spouses. Jennifer has every unmarried man and a few married ones for miles trailing her like puppies. She'll choose soon, I imagine." She smiled and added, "And Jillian, well, she is lively and bright and especially beautiful, even for our family."

What an odd woman, he thought. No reaction visible except when she mentions her younger sister. And her opinion of herself was skewed. "You are a very beautiful woman, Julia. I can hardly believe you don't realize that."

She looked him square in the eye. "No need to do that," she said.

Jake sat back in his chair. "Do what?"

47

"It is really unnecessary."

"I don't know what you're talking about. You're a very attractive woman. Not that that sort of thing matters much to me or anyone in my family. But still I have eyes in my head," Jake said.

"Tell me about your family, Jake. About your sisters. I can hardly imagine them welcoming me when I am nearly stealing their inheritance, but still if I knew something about them, I could smooth the way."

His bride's face was flushed and having only known her for a short time, he wasn't positive, but he would have guessed she was spitting mad. Not many women of his acquaintance took exception to a compliment. It was then he realized what she had said. "Stealing their inheritance?" he repeated.

"This land. The farm. If you hadn't married, they'd be entitled to part of it."

Jake was more than a little irritated that his new bride would think so little of his sisters without even having met them. "They have farms of their own. I told you I helped Flossie and Gloria both when they got married. They don't think of my bride as stealing their inheritance. What a damn fool thing to say."

"Obviously you know little about woman, Mr. Shelling," she replied.

Jake stood and looked down at her, angry. "I know my sisters, Julia. I raised them. They could care less about their 'inheritance.'"

"I didn't mean to insult you or your sisters. It's just that I know how women's minds work. What's important to them. Not that it's all so important to me but still I understand," she replied.

Jake would have asked what was important to woman if he hadn't heard the wagons pulling into the yard. This was going to be awkward to be sure, and he had less a clear idea of his wife now then the moment he'd slipped the ring on her finger. He stood and looked out the kitchen window.

"They're here."

* * * *

Julia's stomach rolled. She prayed these sisters didn't care about their inheritance. About a woman who married the first man she saw when she got off the train. About a woman running from herself and her sister's husband. Not that they'd ever know that story, but still, Julia knew it. She stood straightened her dress and wished she'd taken time to wipe the dust from her face and hands. The screen door in the kitchen flew open with a bang. Jake crouched down, and two dark-haired children ran into his arms. He stood, pretended to stagger, and they giggled.

Jake kissed both children. "I suppose you're mad at your Uncle Jake cause your mother kept you home from the Founder's Day Celebration to meet my bride."

"We were," the boy said. "But we're not anymore. Mama said your new wife talks different than us."

"And she came from far, far away just to marry you," the little girl said while covering Jake's face with kisses. "I told Mama I would a married you."

"You're going to meet a man a lot better looking than your Uncle Jake one of these days." Jake slid the children down his body to the floor. He turned them to face Julia. "These are my sister Flossie and her husband Harry's kids. Danny is seven and Millie is five. This is your Aunt Julia."

Both children looked up at 'him in confusion. The door opened again, and two women and two men came into the kitchen. Before Julia's husband could explain further, one of the women waddled over to her.

"Hel-lo." She smiled and pointed a finger at her chest as she shouted. "Gloria."

"She's foreign, not deaf," the younger of the two men said.

Julia looked at the smiling pregnant woman. Her husband's youngest sister, she imagined. She had the same dark hair as Jake and big green eyes. Her husband was probably the blonde and handsome one. All Julia could think of was that their children would be beautiful, like William. But before she could speak, the other woman approached. She was thinner-faced and would have been passably attractive but for a huge scar that ran from her eye to her mouth. The tightened skin made her bottom lip turn down on one side. Her eyes, though, Julia thought were the happiest she'd ever seen. Julia fought to keep from staring at the disfigurement.

The woman took Julia's hand and smiled. "Inga, I want to welcome you to our family. I'm Flossie, and that's my husband Harry. Gloria's the one who screamed in your ear, and that's her husband Will. I imagine you already met the kids. They ran in ahead of us." Flossie turned to Jake. "Do you think she's getting any of this?"

Danny pulled on his mother's skirt. "Her name's not Inga, Ma."

"Why doesn't everybody sit down," Jake said. "There's something I've got to explain. Come sit down, Julia."

"Julia!"

"I thought you said her name was Inga?"

"I told ya, Ma."

Julia sat down at the seat Jake indicated. He stood behind her. Flossie and Harry sat on the right. Gloria and Will on Julia's left. The children stood between their mother and father.

"With the Founder's Day Celebration there was a lot of confusion and noise at the station." Jake tapped Julia's shoulders. "This is, was Miss Crawford not Miss Crawper. She corresponded with Jacob Snelling and came here to marry him."

"So what happened?" Gloria asked. "Where is Miss Crawper? From Sweden."

"As you know I took Pastor Phillips to the station with me. In all that confusion and noise I married Miss Crawford from Boston, not Miss Crawper," Jake said.

Flossie whispered the conclusion. "Jake Shelling."

Julia did not realize the situation could sound worse than it was. But it did. Jake's sisters and the children stared at her and Jake alternately. His brothers-in-law looked at each other and then stood simultaneously. Will followed Harry out the door. Julia had no idea why until she heard their muffled laughter.

"Sorry," Flossie muttered.

Gloria leaned forward and covered Julia's hand with her own. "You ought to thank your lucky stars that station was busy." She scrunched her face in disgust. "Jacob Snelling *and* his mother. Yee gads." Gloria brightened. "Yes, you certainly were lucky the station was busy."

"What happened to Miss Crawper?" Flossie asked.

"She and Mr. Snelling may have come to an understanding," Julia said.

"And we know what the understanding will be," Gloria said. "Wait on old Mrs. Snelling and listen to her complain."

"Gloria!" Flossie said.

"It's true. You know it's true, Flossie."

Flossie tilted her head towards Julia and looked at Gloria. "She was Mr. Snelling's fiancé. Try and consider Miss Crawford's feelings." Flossie faced Julia. "I imagine this has been quite a day for you. And not all good. Other than marrying my brother, of course."

"It has been a very trying day," Julia said.

Will and Harry came in the kitchen and turned around just as quickly and ran outside. Flossie smiled at

Julia as their laughter rang through the kitchen. "Our husbands have taken great joy from Jake's marriage pursuits."

"Pursuits?" Julia asked. She looked up over her shoulder to Jake's face. "Have you been married before?"

Before Jake could answer, Flossie stood and pointed to Julia's trunks in the hallway. "You're not even settled." Flossie yelled out the open window. "Will, Harry, come carry Julia's things upstairs."

Chapter Five

JULIA WAS USHERED UP A dark staircase. Will and Harry carried her trunks and bags. The men left the room as quickly as they entered leaving Julia alone with her new sisters-in-law. A light colored quilt covered the bed. Flossie was busy opening windows and pulling back curtains.

"This was my room, growing up," Gloria said. "Seems like a hundred years ago."

"You've been married and out of this room less than a year," Flossie said.

Gloria trailed her hand over the spread on the bed. She seated herself with a groan and looked at Julia. "Do you like it?"

"It's very nice."

Nothing like her room back at home but still sunny and pleasant. Julia wanted to blurt out questions about her new husband but opted instead to smile pleasantly as if she moved into a new state, a new home and married the wrong man everyday.

"Jake wasn't married before," Flossie said and told a story about a woman named Valerie Morton to Julia.

"Jake's a wonderful man. The best brother, the best uncle but he's not inclined to trust or forgive mistakes easily. Especially ones he makes," Flossie said. "I suppose 'cause he had to grow up so quick when Ma and Pa died. Mistakes could cost crops or livestock or a life out here."

"I'm a mistake then?" Julia asked.

"I don't think so. But I'll bet he's rethinking taking the minister to the train station," Flossie said. "More so cause I was here this morning trying to talk him out of it."

"I wish you'd succeeded," Julia said. She looked at the uncomfortable faces before her. "I didn't mean any insult to your brother, but it is quite a drastic change in my plans."

Flossie sat down beside her. "Tell us your plans. What brought you all the way here to marry Mr. Snelling?"

"Well," Julia said, blushing, "I imagine that's obvious. I am twenty-seven."

"You felt you had to come to South Dakota to marry?" Gloria asked. "Weren't there any men in Boston to marry?"

Flossie laughed. "You sound as if you're asking if there were chickens to buy, Gloria. Maybe Julia didn't like any of the men in Boston."

"You know what I mean. And anyway," Gloria said as she picked up the edge of Julia's gown, "looks like your folks were comfortable. Weren't there parties and what not?"

"Many parties. But I was hardly the belle of ball," Julia said. "I have three sisters."

"Not the belle of the ball? With your hair and clothes? You're so pretty. There must have been plenty of men interested," Gloria said.

"That's kind of you to say," Julia said. It had been a while since she heard such a sentiment. And spoken honestly like Jillian or Eustace would have done. "My sister's are very beautiful. Suitors seem to flock their way."

Flossie let out a deep sigh. "Well, this is hardly what you planned. But as for Jake's plans, it isn't much different than he intended."

"He was going to marry a woman he had never met. Knew nothing about. That's what I've gathered from his comments and yours. Is it true?" Julia asked.

"That pretty much sums it up," Gloria said, shaking her head.

Julia wondered about the man that was to be her husband for better or worse. He would be satisfied knowing nothing about his lifetime mate before marriage.

"I find it hard to imagine marrying someone I know nothing about." Julia turned and stared out the window. "Although that is exactly what I've done." Flossie picked up her hand and squeezed.

"You have to understand Jake to understand why he was willing to marry this way. When our parents died, he was just sixteen-years-old, I was nine and Gloria was three. Mother and Father had bought this land sight unseen. They had some money to build a house and hire some men to get the lands cleared, but they died within the first year. The hands Father had hired ran off, and no one would work for us. Three kids really. I begged Jake to sell the land and move to town. But he'd have none of it. And now I'm glad he held his ground."

Flossie paused and stared, obviously remembering those first hard years. "But I'm off the subject. You see, Jake spent his life raising us, working the farm, worrying about money and crops. He never went to a dance or a social. He made sure we went and had a new dress too, but he never went himself. I don't think he has any idea what love or marriage is about. Jake gets an idea in his head figures out how to do it and just does it. This time the idea was a bride."

"That's Jake all right," Gloria said. "I told him he couldn't get a bride like he buys a new mare or haggles over another piece of land. He just wouldn't listen."

"I think I understand," Julia said.

"You won't understand for awhile. Till you get to know Jake." Flossie said. "He told me right after Gloria got married it was time for him to marry. Time for a son to pass his land to and a helpmate. And he certainly won't admit it, but he's lonely."

"And just about anyone willing would do," Julia added.

Gloria laughed. "There were lots willing. Trust me. Plenty of women were interested in Jake, but they grew tired of waiting and most married. 'Cept Clara. Cripes, Flossie, wait till Clara hears about this."

"Jake wasn't interested in Clara even when Jake decided to marry," Flossie said.

"Who's Clara?" Julia asked.

"Clara Fawcett. Her father owns the bank in town. She wears clothes ordered from back east. Her hair's always just so. She never leaves her house without gloves." Gloria flitted both hands. "Jake knew right off she wasn't the kind of woman to help run a farm. Too fancy and fussy."

Clara sounded like everything Julia was accustomed to. "And she wanted to marry Jake?"

"Clara just wasn't suited for Jake. She was the only one that couldn't see it," Flossie said.

Julia stared at her hands and lifted her head slowly to look at her new family. "So what you're saying is Jake decided one day to marry, anyone, even someone he never met and a respectable woman from his own town would have married him, and he didn't want her because she wasn't meant for life on a farm. And she's someone just like me."

Gloria covered her hand with her mouth. "You're right."

"Gloria," Flossie said sharply. "We don't know anything about Julia. How could we think she's the same as Clara?"

"Well, look at her clothes and hat and such, Flossie. Jake's going to have a fit when he realizes," Gloria said.

"Does everything that comes into your head have to come flying out of your mouth?" Flossie asked.

"From the sounds of it I'm exactly what your brother did not want in a wife," Julia said.

Flossie stood and faced the women still seated on the bed. "Now you two listen to me. I didn't agree with Jake's plan. Marrying isn't like picking a prize sow. But what's done is done. Julia, if you're going to stick this out, you better make the best of it. Gloria and I will help. Is this what you want, Julia?"

Julia knew the woman was right. If she had any intention of beginning a new life, then she'd best do all she could. She didn't know where to start but Jake's sister's said they'd help. "I don't want a divorce. What's done is done. I'll make the best of the circumstances."

"Are you sure?" Gloria asked. "You sure you don't want to go home?"

"No. I don't want to go home," Julia said.

"Was it so bad there?" Flossie asked. "Some folks will gladly take the devil they know rather than the devil they don't."

"I'm twenty-seven. I'm the fat, unattractive spinster in a family of beautiful women. I've made some bad decisions and been an embarrassment to them all of my life. My plan to marry Mr. Snelling was an opportunity for me to do something on my own. I don't want to go back. I won't go back, especially with my head bowed in shame," Julia said.

The confession said aloud was liberating for Julia. She had no idea why she was inclined to share these long silent burdens with strangers, but it felt good. She had been honest with herself and Jake's sisters. She didn't want to go home. They were staring at her intensely. She wondered if the women realized Julia would be taking a slice of their and their children's birthright with her adamant declaration.

"I'm not sure why you're willing to help me. My marriage will take your inheritance from your brother's farm away from you and your family, but if you're willing regardless, I'll be happy to accept the help."

"You said a mouthful there, and I'm pretty sure you don't usually share your feelings," Flossie said. "I can speak for Gloria though when I tell you we don't give a damn about an inheritance. We got our share when we married, and Jake's got the right to pass his share on to his wife or children or whoever he wants."

"Why would we want part of Jake's farm? We have our own," Gloria added.

"Women have no way of gaining wealth unless it's passed on. You can hardly say you don't care you'll be losing what could be a portion of a profitable property as well as the home you were raised in."

Julia learned that lesson well from her sister. When her grandfather died, the only thing of interest to her was the broken gold timepiece he always carried with him, and that had fascinated her as a child. Jolene and her mother had the estate manager sell the grandparents' gifts to the Crawford girls to increase the size of their dowry. Julia had been crushed.

Flossie sat down beside Julia. "What kind of family did you come from?"

Julia looked from Flossie to Gloria. "What do you mean? I guess a normal family. Not that I always agreed with them. But I know about losing a birthright. I'll likely never see the inheritance I would have meant to receive once my family finds out I've taken a train to South Dakota and married."

Gloria's eyes widened. "Your folks don't know you came out here to marry Mr. Snelling?"

Julia could have bit her tongue off. But the truth was out now. "Our maid, my friend, Eustace will give everyone a letter day after tomorrow. They think I went to visit an elderly aunt."

"This is just like one of my books," Gloria said. "The frightened girl sneaks out of the castle in the middle of the night. Jake can be your knight in shining armor."

"Be quiet, Gloria." Flossie turned to Julia. "So when your parents find out, they'll be angry?"

"Angry and embarrassed but this is no less than they expect from me," Julia said. She looked at her new sisters-in-law as the family she'd always hoped to have. "My father will surely send someone here to get me. Or maybe even come himself. Will Jake let them take me?"

"You're his wife, Julia. What's Jake's stays Jake's. If you don't want to go back, he'll not let your family bother you," Flossie said.

Julia dropped her head. "My father can be very persuasive when he sets his mind to it."

"There'll be no persuading, Julia. If you want to stay, Jake can't be bought if that's what you're implying. He's the most honorable, honest man I know," Flossie said.

"That's twice today I've heard that about him."

"It's true." Gloria added with a smile. "Jake can't abide lies. And you're his wife now, he'll guard you like family. You are family. Like me and Flossie and the kids."

Julia smiled back at her sister-in-law. What a comforting thought to part a family. She had allies. Julia decided then and there she wanted to be part of the Shelling family nearly more than anything she ever wanted. And she was going to do what was necessary to make them proud. "I imagine the gentlemen are wondering where we're at. We've been up here a long time."

Gloria stood slowly. "No. Harry and Will will say, 'So that's your new bride.' Jake will say 'yep', and they'll take the kids out to the barn or look at some fencing."

Julia laughed. So did Flossie.

"You're right about that. But we still have lots to do. We have to get Julia here unpacked and think about supper and getting her started tomorrow," Flossie said as she stood.

Julia looked up at them and smiled with less anxiety and more hope than she'd felt in a long while. "Thank you."

* * *

Gloria threw together biscuits and Flossie found a piece of ham hanging in the smoke house. Julia watched as the two women made a thick white gravy with the ham drippings. She burnt herself twice on the stove and resigned herself to setting the table. Gloria promised to bring by her recipe box the next week for Julia to copy. Flossie said she'd help her clean the kitchen and unpack. The Shelling family crowded around the table, and Jake said grace. The women's work was devoured in moments. But the family laughed and talked about everyday things until someone mentioned Julia. The table's occupants quieted, and some nodded politely at her, as if unsure of what to make of Jake's new wife. Well, she didn't blame them; she didn't know what to make of herself.

Her new husband was clearly the head of the Shelling family. Will and Harry deferred to him and asked his advice. His niece and nephew hung on every word out of his mouth. And his sisters visibly adored him. And he them. There were only warm looks and words between them all. Julia felt like an outsider knowing little of what they discussed, but she saw a better chance of belonging than at any time in her life. The teasing hope of happiness was present, and Julia was determined to be part of it.

She stood beside Jake on the porch and waved goodbye to his sisters and their husbands. Flossie, Gloria and his niece and nephew had kissed him goodbye and told him they loved him. He kissed them back and returned the sentiment. Millie waved goodbye from the back of the wagon long after Julia could see her face. She looked up at her husband.

"Your family is all very kind. They made me feel welcome."

Chapter Six

KNEW THEY WOULD," JAKE SAID. He looked down at the beautiful blonde that was now his bride. "They like you already."

Julia folded her hands at her waist. "I'm glad. I like them."

The unasked and unanswered question was whether or not Julia liked him as well. Will and Harry had twisted and squirmed in their skin for want of asking questions. He knew what they were thinking. He had ordered a workhorse and got a hothouse flower.

Like a daffodil in April, Julia was fresh and delicate. But clueless as to farm life, even he could see that. All done up in layers of yellow, nearly matching the blonde of her hair. Her eyes were as clear blue as the sky on a summer morning. His new bride was like a bouquet of colors in contrast to his dark hair and the tan skin of his face and hands.

"I 'spect you're tired. I'll heat water so you can wash up."

"Would you mind if we sat and talked?" she asked.

"No. I imagine we've got some things to work out," Jake replied as he opened the screen door to let her pass.

"Work out?" she repeated.

Jake pulled a bottle of whiskey from under the sink and poured himself two fingers full in a small glass before sitting down across from Julia.

"Yeah, work out. What we do here on the farm. What's expected of you. What you can expect of me." His bride's hands were shaking, and she was eying his glass of sour mash. "Would you like some?" Jake asked as he lifted his glass.

"Yes, please."

Jake handed her a glass of whiskey. "I'm usually up by four or four-thirty. Not much to be done in the fields till harvest, but me and the boys work getting the barns and silos ready. Mend fences, that sort of thing."

"I was hoping to talk about something of a more personal nature," Julia said.

Jake hoped this wasn't going to be a list of things he was supposed to do like wearing a tie to church and dabbing a napkin on his mouth when he got egg yolk on his chin.

"Like what?" he asked.

"I was wondering why Flossie and Gloria didn't put my things in your bedroom."

Of all the things Julia could have said, Jake expected this question the least. He had conceded to Flossie's wishes and agreed to get to know his new bride before bedding her.

"I thought maybe we could take some time getting to know each other."

"Are you," she said and stopped to clear her throat, "are you saying you think we should wait?"

Julia was looking at the wall just past his left shoulder. "You're a beautiful woman, Julia. I've already told you that. But considering how things began," he trailed off.

She looked him in the eye. "I think we should consummate the marriage."

Jake stared at his glass and swirled the amber liquor. "I'll admit, I wouldn't mind, but I was figuring . . ."

"My family doesn't know I came here to marry. They think I'm visiting my Aunt Mildred. I'm not a virgin."

Jake leaned his forearms on the table, hands clasped. He knew something was behind a woman this beautiful leaving her rich Boston family for the prairie and Jacob Snelling. He wanted to know now rather than later exactly the kind of woman he'd married. Maybe it was too late to forestall a visit from a lawman out of Boston.

"S'pose you could elaborate, Julia. On both things if you don't mind."

"What do you want to hear about first?" she asked.

"Either," Jake said.

"My family thinks I left four days ago from Boston to visit my Aunt Mildred. My father's mother's sister. I left letters for my family. Eustace, our maid, is going to hand them out next Friday and then, well, then they will know I didn't go to Delaware."

"And in those letters you tell your family you came to South Dakota to marry Jacob Snelling."

"Yes."

"What's going to happen when your family finds out you're not in Delaware?" Jake asked.

She stared at her hands folded around her glass of whiskey. "My mother and father will be very unhappy." She looked at Jake. "I imagine my father will send someone immediately to take me back to Boston."

Jake linked his hands behind his head and tilted his chair back. There was some deceit going on here, of that Jake was sure. "So if we go to bed now, I won't let him take you."

"Something like that," she said.

This woman had as many layers as an onion, and if he wasn't careful, he'd end up with tears in his eyes. He'd didn't give a rat's ass about her family sending someone after her. She was his wife, now, for better or for worse. And after a long time without a woman, he wasn't inclined to turn down her offer. Regardless of what her reasoning was. In either case, they were married. He'd made his bed by dragging the minister to the train station that morning.

"And the other?"

Her lips were quivering. "Well, I imagined you'd figure the second thing out if we went ahead with the first and I didn't want to be dishonest."

"What did you tell Snelling?" he asked.

She dropped her head. "That I was a widow."

Jake poured himself another glassful of whiskey and refilled Julia's. "You lied to him. Why not tell me the same story?" he said.

"He was different."

Jake harrumphed. "I imagine he's got the same thing as every other man."

"I imagine he does. But that marriage was about companionship and company for his mother. I just didn't think he'd ever know," she whispered.

"And I would?" he asked.

"After I thought about things, meeting your family and everything, I decided I wanted to try, really try to be happy and make a husband happy. I don't imagine that would go so well if I lied. It would always be between us. I know you weren't looking for a grand love affair, but you're close to my age. We'll be together for many years," Julia said.

"And since Jacob's near sixty, you were hoping he'd kick off before your conscience got hold of you," Jake said.

"That's not a very nice way to put it, but I suppose it's accurate."

"Who was he?" Jake asked.

"Pardon?" Julia said, eyes wide. She lowered her head. "It was a long, long time ago. You wouldn't know him."

"I realize that Julia. But you're my wife. I have a right to know."

"Do I have a right to know every woman you've ever been with?" she said and raised her chin.

"If you want to know, I'll tell you. The list is short. Most of whom were paid for. Do you want me to name names?" Jake replied. She sat silently so long; Jake was convinced she wasn't going to reply.

"Turner Crenshaw," she said finally.

Jake was confused. He could have sworn Julia mentioned that name when she was talking about her family. "Didn't you say . . ."

"Yes. He's my sister's husband. It happened before Jolene and he married. I was seventeen."

This confession had cost his new bride. She was staring out the kitchen door, apparently not willing to meet his eyes. Her profile was a picture of misery and guilt. Her pain and the shimmer of tears on her lashes, was wending its way into Jake's middle. It was alive, thriving and tearing this woman apart.

"Do you still love him?"

She turned to him. Her lip was quivering. "Why would a woman love a man who doesn't want her? Why would anyone put herself through that kind of misery year after year? How does she get through the sister's wedding? Why would she still love him, seeing him day in and day out, worshipping the ground beneath the feet of another woman?"

She wasn't talking about some poor faceless pathetic stranger. She was talking about herself and her hurt was raw and pulsing and still fresh.

"I don't know, Julia. How did you do it all?" Jake asked.

"I put it all aside. I put it all aside for my family's sake. So there would be no shame, no whisper of a scandal." Julia said, her voice raised and quivering. "He took one look at Jolene and walked away from as if he'd never met me. Never touched me," she whispered. "She was the oldest, my mother said. Said Jolene deserved him. She went to him a virgin on her wedding night. Something I could never do."

Jake stood and went to Julia. He pulled her up from her chair and put his hands on her shoulders. "Your mother shouldn't have said that. She should have never have said any of that."

She looked up at him. "Why? It's all true."

"Bullshit, Julia. Your father should have hog-tied him and dragged him to the altar. You were a young girl. You made a mistake. He took advantage. They shouldn't have wanted a piece of crap like Turner Crenshaw to marry any of their daughters. Let alone make you stand up for your sister," Jake said.

He was mad as hell. He could have never been so cruel to his sisters, and he wondered what kind of parent could be. Julia was shaking all over.

"So you see I can never go back. I can't take it. I don't love him anymore, haven't for a long while, but seeing him everyday, with his son, with Jolene. They won't let me forget."

Jake pulled her into his arms. She laid her head on his chest and he rubbed slow circles on her back.

"South Dakota's a new start for you. Put it behind you." He pushed her back in his arms to look her in the eye. "But I don't want my wife pining all her life for some man not worthy to shine her shoes. I mean it, Julia. We're married."

She nodded. "I want to start over. I'm going to do my best to be a good wife."

Jake pulled her back against his chest. She felt good there. Smelled good too, even after a day like they'd had. Jake chuckled.

"This is why I want sons. Went through worrying about this stuff with Flossie and Gloria. Don't know if I could take it with a daughter." He pushed her away from his chest holding her in a loose hug and smiled a lopsided grin. "That's why I ordered Inga. She had eight brothers. I figured that was as good chance as any of having boys."

As quick as lightening, Julia's face went from smiling and relaxed to a shy rosy pink color. *She wants this. I want this. Ah, hell, might as well see if the kissing will make me want to hurry or dawdle.* If he should put his silver on the nightstand before the deed so he wouldn't have to face a woman he didn't know, but had bedded. Or if by some stroke of luck, he would want to be in that bed every night. Jake tilted her chin up with his finger and touched her lips with his. His eyes closed of their own volition. Not because he didn't want to see the rouge lined face of a soiled dove either. They just closed, as if any distraction would take away the pure pleasure he was feeling.

Jake reached behind him and pulled a kitchen chair out. He eased down onto it and pulled Julia into his lap as he did. He was thinking dawdling would do just fine as far as kissing his wife was concerned. Her head tilted back over his arm as he turned to deepen the kiss. Jake didn't know how long they sat on the kitchen chair. Could have been months for all he cared. She seemed to be enjoying herself as much as he was and he figured now was as good a time as any to carry her upstairs. Jake broke away from her lips but stayed inches from her face.

* * *

It had been a long time since a man had kissed her. He was trembling as much as she. Julia sent a fleeting prayer aloft that he would find her as attractive as she found him. Maybe her morals were as loose as her mother claimed, she thought, as a sigh rolled up within her. *Quit thinking, Julia. Feel and enjoy. This could have been Jacob Snelling.* Julia touched the dark hair along his collar.

"We can wait, Julia. Are you sure you want to do this your first day here," he asked.

He was giving her a choice. But did she really want to stop? She was aching in the pit of her stomach for a man she didn't even know. Fear had turned to anticipation with Jake's kisses.

"I don't want to wait," she said.

Jake eased her from his lap and stood up. "I'll leave you to wash up and what not," he said as he twirled his hat in his hand. "Be back up to the house in an hour or so."

Years ago, Julia had eavesdropped on Jolene as her sister and a married friend were talking. Jolene had described suffering the marriage bed dutifully. And that Turner was after her near every night. But she would put a stop to that, Jolene had confided to the woman. Her disinterest and their forthcoming child would slacken his lust. Jolene had laughed her throaty laugh. That or separate bedrooms would, Jolene had said. How her sister could have not wanted Turner's attentions were beyond her.

And Jake Shelling was a handsome man. Every edge was hard other than his brown hair. It looked like silk shimmering in the gaslight. He was tall. Probably a good foot or more taller than her. Somehow it was comforting to think of her husband as being taller than her father. His eyes were green, clear and direct.

If her and Jake's marriage were consummated, her father would have few rights. Just in case, contrary to Flossie and his own assurances, her new husband didn't feel inclined to keep what was his, his.

For a moment Julia let herself return to that moment that altered her life so drastically. So different than what she prepared for in the present. She could swear she smelled honeysuckle climbing the trellis behind the house. Turner's attention that evening at the party of a friends' had been too much of a lure. Too much of an affirmation that she too was attractive. Things had gone farther than they should have quickly. He had not spoken to another soul at the party once he had been introduced to her. His attention was like a drug. Addicting and never fully satisfying. Ten years was a long time to wait for her next kiss.

But Jake's kisses were worth the wait. Not as much as his words, though. No one, *no one*, had ever defended her before. No one had made Turner bear any of the blame. Until Jake. His kisses made her feel wanted and beautiful. Jake had heard her tale and instead of being outraged that he'd married a woman like her, he'd managed to find a way to substantiate his reasoning for wanting sons rather than daughters.

She slipped a sheer white, lace-edged nightgown over her head and pulled on the matching robe. Julia pulled the ribbon across her bosom and tied a bow. She looked in the mirror over a stand holding a razor and brush. The low-neck line of the gown and the bow brought her eyes to her bulging cleavage. Her best attribute as far as she was concerned. She dabbed cologne behind her ears and brushed her hair till it shone. I feel pretty; she thought and batted her lashes as she had seen Jennifer do. Julia was confident as she climbed the steps to Jake's room. That confidence ebbed as she pulled back the covers of her husband's bed and climbed in to wait. But she did not wait long.

Chapter Seven

"COME IN," JULIA SAID TO Jake's knock.

"You are quite a beautiful woman, Julia," he said as stood in the doorway and stared unashamedly.

Julia watched Jake's Adam's apple bob while he gawked at the bow of her robe. She shimmied down under the sheet. He wanted her; that was certain. She watched him slowly unbutton his shirt. His chest was broad and muscular. He was staring at her like Alred McClintok looked at his plate of shrimp. She squirmed as he pulled his pants down over narrow hips. Her one sexual encounter had been in the dark and the sun, while already set, still lit the room softly. She could see clearly.

"Oh dear," was all she could say.

"I don't want to do anything you don't want me to do. Just say the word and I'll stop," Jake said as he pulled back the covers on his side of the bed.

Julia dropped her lashes, oddly unafraid. Here she was far from home and family in the bed of a stranger, her new husband, and she was not the least bit frightened. He was a big man, in girth and depth, and it attracted her more than scared her.

"I did like when you kissed me, Jake. Maybe we should start there."

Jake slipped under the covers and slid his arm under her neck. He settled her on his shoulder and touched his lips to hers. He kissed her ear, and she moaned and moved closer, her breasts to his chest, her knees at his thighs, her toes tickling his shins. Jake slowly pulled the ribbon of her robe open. He growled.

This man was big everywhere. It was heaven, Julia thought. Big enough to keep her father or the bogeyman at bay. Big enough to drown in and feel dainty. She slid her fingers down his side to rest on his hip. He was kissing her neck, her shoulders. Julia felt his hand encompass her breast. A low moan rumbled from his chest.

Jake looked her in the eye. "It's been a long time for me. I don't think I can wait much longer."

"It's been a long time for me, too." Julia's eyes opened at half-mast, struggling to focus on the man's face before her as his hand kneaded her breast, and he ran a calloused thumb over her nipple.

Her husband inched the gossamer gown over her hips and rolled her onto her back. He slid his hand up a thigh and pulled her knee up and around his hip and eased into her with one, long, slow stroke. His eyes fluttered, and he hummed a contented murmur as he sunk into her body.

They were like chocolate truffles and champagne, Julia thought. Two unrelated items, no one dreamed would go together. But they did. Edgy pings of bubbles against creamy softness. She opened her eyes and tilted her head back to see her husband's face. Which was he? Candy or champagne? Both, she decided. He was staring at her, questions in his gaze. Julia put her hands on his cheeks, smoothly shaved, and kissed him, touching her tongue to his.

Apparently it was all the answer he needed. Jake slid himself in and out of her body and ran his knuckles against the side of her breast and down to her waist. He linked his fingers with hers and held her hand against the pillow beside her head. The tide of completion seemed to rush at him, and his tempo increased. Julia met him halfway with every thrust. She trailed the palms of her feet over his calves, and Jake groaned and settled on her.

As her breathing stilled, Julia ran her hands up Jake's back. Maybe Eustace was right. Things were going to work out just fine. Had someone told her yesterday she'd be in bed with a giant man and loving every minute of it, she'd have sworn they were insane. The mousy, fat, spinster Crawford girl had made love to a gorgeous man.

Her husband. A shiver of pleasure and surprise at her response to Jake's touch trailed down her arms.

Jake rolled on his side. He propped himself on one elbow beside her. "Are you cold?"

Julia smiled shyly. "Not at all."

He trailed a finger down her cheek and twisted it in her hair. "That was pretty wonderful from my point of view."

Her lashes dropped half way. She was desirable, a vixen, a temptress.

"Perfectly wonderful. I think we may suit admirably, Mr. Shelling."

"No question about that, Mrs. Shelling. No question at all," Jake said and stared at her.

* * *

Julia awoke as the sun streamed in her window. Jake was not there. They had slept together all night. She washed and rooted through clothes for something cool and suitable for life on a farm. She had nothing. Julia pulled on the plainest dress she owned over one petticoat. It was white eyelet with flounces of ruffles with a high neck and full sleeves that narrowed to tight cuffs. Julia struggled with the eight covered buttons on each wrist. She brushed out her hair and pulled it into a matching ribbon. She pinched her cheeks and went down stairs. Jake walked in the backdoor as she entered the kitchen. Flossie was at the table, rolling out bread dough.

"I'm sorry. I didn't realize you were here already. What time is it?" Julia asked.

"Nearly eight o'clock." Flossie looked up from her kneading and smiled. "I got here about six-thirty. Wanted to let you sleep in your first day. I just went ahead and started, hope you don't mind."

"Were you up early as well?" Julia asked Jake as she seated herself.

Jake smiled. "Sunrise. I wanted to let you sleep."

"Oh," she said. She had awoken in the middle of the night as Jake kissed her neck and cupped her breast. Their lovemaking had been frantic, leaving them both panting. She had fallen back asleep sprawled across him.

Jake poured himself a cup of coffee, walked to her and kissed her on the lips. Her face heated with a blush. She couldn't look at Flossie. He kissed her again and then pulled out a chair and pushed it close to straddle it beside her.

"Want some coffee?" he asked.

"I'll get it." Julia stared at her husband. He looked smug. And cocky. And adorable for a man twice her size. She grinned, plopped her hand on her chin and rolled her eyes.

"I'm right here. Still in the kitchen if you two hadn't noticed," Flossie said.

Without turning from Julia's face, Jake answered his sister. "We know."

Julia dropped her head and cleared her throat. "I've never made bread before. Would you teach me, Flossie?"

Jake lowered his voice to a whisper. "I'll teach you anything you need to know, Julia."

"I'm talking to your sister," she said.

"I know," Jake said with a smile.

Flossie looked from her brother to her new sister-in-law and back. "I guess taking the time to get to know each other fell by the way side."

"We got to know . . ." Jake began.

Julia jumped from her chair. "What do you do next, Flossie?" Julia said and pointed at the bread dough.

Flossie looked at Jake, cut off mid-sentence by his wife. "We're going to let the dough rest for awhile. Thought maybe you'd like some help unpacking and cleaning."

Jake rose slowly. "I'm going out to the barn. Holler if you need me."

It was all Julia could do to look Flossie in the eye. When she did, she realized Flossie was staring. Julia glanced away absently.

"I didn't think I'd live to see the day. My brother mooning over a woman. And in front of me yet," Flossie said.

Julia looked at her hands. "I would hardly call it mooning."

"Well, something's different about him. Kissing you and trying to make us both uncomfortable. Jake Shelling doesn't tease or kid. Other than with Millie or Danny. Something's different."

Julia looked at her slack-jawed sister-in-law. "He's always serious then?"

"Not anymore."

"None of my clothes seem appropriate for life here. I sew a fair needlepoint stitch but never made any clothes. Should I ask Jake if I could buy some fabric or cut down the clothes I have?" Julia asked.

"Having been married some years now, I'd get to Snelling's store and pick out anything you want. Chances are good right now that Jake'd buy every bolt Snelling had in stock," Flossie said. "Harry and I have to go into town tomorrow. Want to ride along?"

Julia smiled. "Yes, I would enjoy that."

Flossie gathered a bucket and rags and together they gave Jake's house the scrubbing it needed. Soon Julia's white dress was covered in dirt. Her last nail had broken and cobwebs were stuck in her hair. Julia thanked God when Flossie announced they would take a break from cleaning and put her things away. Julia pulled her trunks down the hall from Gloria's old room to Jake's. Flossie did not say a word on the room adjustment but marveled over Julia's lace gloves and dresses. They arranged some of Julia's wardrobe in Jake's tiny cupboard. The fanciest they left in her trunk for storage. As Julia and Flossie went down the steps Julia realized there were still buckets of dirty scrub water in the hallway, yet to be dumped. Clean walls met dirty with a clear demarcation.

"Lordy, is it that the time already," Flossie said as she looked at the watch pinned to her dress. "The kids'll be hungry, and Harry will have a fit if I'm not home soon."

Julia's stomach growled. "Hurry home then. You've been a great help."

"We didn't get anything ready for supper," Flossie said.

"I'll manage," Julia replied with a smile.

"Pick you up early, like about seven o'clock in the morning, Julia. Harry hates to head to town late in the day when it's crowded," Flossie said as she went out the door.

Julia waved goodbye to Flossie. She pulled back a curtain hanging in the corner of the kitchen where Jake said shelves were filled with supplies. Certainly there would be something here she could make. She gathered more potatoes in her arms than she could carry and headed to the sink. Potatoes slipped away as she hurried and hit the floor with a thud.

Julia rinsed what she still held and put them in a pot on the stove to boil. She stoked the stove as Flossie had shown her. She lugged the heavy buckets of filthy water to the door of the kitchen but could get no further. Julia filled the sink with tepid water from the warming reservoir on the back of the stove and unbuttoned her cuffs. She struggled with buttons on the back of her dress. Julia swore she would only have dresses with front buttons now that she had no maid. She stood at the sink, dress around her waist, in her silk chemise and washed.

* * *

Jake came up from the barn to get a cool drink and see if Julia still looked as pretty as he remembered from that morning and as tempting as she had the night before. His bride was as soft as newborn chick down and all woman that was for certain, every curvy indent, every rounded bit of flesh. Jake had been scared to death he'd crush her when they made love. She was such little thing, tucked under him, mewing soft sounds of pleasure. He was thinking it would only get better with time and familiarity. If it could.

He stopped dead in his tracks at his screen door. Julia stood in front of the sink, hair pulled up except for a few tendrils stuck wet to her back. Her dress was to her waist and she was running a washrag over her neck. Her skin was as pale as the shiny fabric of her underclothes. Julia tilted her head from side to side and hummed softly. Jake turned quickly when he heard his foreman hollering to him. He slammed the kitchen door open prepared to ask his bride what in the hell she thought she was doing standing near naked within a hundred yards of his randy group of farmhands. She turned as the door swung open. He took one fierce, angry step inside even as the sight of her stirred him.

"What in the hell . . ."

"Be careful," Julia shouted

Jake charged into a bucket of water in front of the door. Water sloshed everywhere and the bucket flew end over end hitting a kitchen chair and knocking it over.

Jake grabbed for the door handle as his feet began to go out from under him. Julia ran to him and kicked an errant potato straight at him. He bent and grabbed his shin where it hit. His muddy boots slipped in the water and sent Jake careening to the floor. He lay still on his back, the wind knocked out of him.

Julia dropped down on her knees beside him.

"Oh, dear. Jake, are you all right?"

It took a moment to get his breath. He could already feel a knot growing on the back of his head. "Julia, everyman jack could a seen you standing at the sink practically naked."

Julia's head popped up to the door. "Does your head hurt? I heard it smack," she asked as she returned her attentions to him.

Julia leaned down close and was running her hand through his hair, bringing her magnificent breasts swinging loosely within inches of his nose.

Julia sat back on her haunches. "No one is looking at me, Jake. What a silly thing to think."

Jake sat up and touched his head gingerly. "Trust me, Julia. The men have been waiting for another glimpse of you since the day I brought you home. If any of them had come on the porch instead of me, they'd a gotten a whole lot more than a glimpse."

She tilted her head. "Don't be angry. I was hot and dirty and wanted to wash up. No one saw me."

Jake straightened out one arm behind him and leaned close to Julia. His eyes dropped to the low scoop of her silk under things and all that beautiful pale flesh behind it. He ran his finger down her neck, to her collarbone and trailed slowly down, stopping when his knuckle touched breast. Julia's eyes dropped, and she let out a slow sigh.

"I know men that'd kill to see a woman like you, looking like this."

"Dinner'll be ready about seven," she whispered and fluttered her lashes.

"What did I trip over anyway?"

"The wash water. I couldn't get any further than the door. It was too heavy. And I dropped a potato on the way to the sink. That's what I kicked when I went to catch you," Julia said.

Jake was sitting in a puddle of foul water on his kitchen floor. His head hurt, and he had hit his behind with a bang. His wife was too weak to carry a bucket of wash water, and his dinner wouldn't be ready till near his bedtime.

"That'll be fine," he said.

"I better get started then," Julia said.

Jake rose, looked her up and down and limped out the door. Julia was a far cry from a thick-waisted, farmwoman from Sweden, but Jake didn't imagine the sight of Inga's broad shoulders would have turned his mind to mush like Julia.

"What happened, Boss?" Slim asked as he limped back into the barn.

"Kicked a bucket of wash water Mrs. Shelling couldn't lift," Jake replied. "I don't want to see my wife carrying anything heavier than her skirts. Got it boys?"

The men smiled and nodded in unison.

* * *

Jake went in the house, near seven o'clock. He'd washed up at the bunkhouse, anticipating sitting down with Julia. And going upstairs with Julia. She wasn't in the kitchen. Julia was slouched awkwardly in one of the horsehair chairs in front of the fireplace. His bride was sound asleep. Instead of being angry the kitchen floor was still damp and the table still unset, Jake tilted his head at the picture before him. She'd tuckered herself out. Cobwebs hung from her curls, and she had missed a spot of dirt on the tip of her nose when she washed. Jake lifted her from the seat into his arms, and she snuggled against him.

Julia woke as Jake lifted her. "There's soup on the counter cooling, Jake. And fresh bread," she whispered.

He kissed the top of her head as he carried her up the steps. "Should a left it on the stove. Stay warm that way."

She yawned. "Potato soup is just as good cold."

Jake didn't have a clue what she was talking about. Who ate their soup cold? And what was he going to eat with it? Was there meat?

"I sugared some berries that Flossie brought." Julia opened her eyes as Jake laid her down on the bed. She sat up and began to unbutton her dress. "No better meal than soup and fresh fruit on a hot day." She smiled up at him lazily as she unpinned her hair.

Jake watched his wife undress. Julia bent down and inched her stockings down her pale legs and her hair swirled around them. She shimmied out of everything but her chemise.

"Think I'll just sleep in this if you don't mind. It's too hot for a nightgown," Julia said. She pulled the sheet up over herself. "I'm so sleepy. I hope you don't mind eating alone. Tell me what you think of the soup. I've watched Cook make it hundreds of times. I think I got it just right."

Jake would have crawled in bed then and there, stomach growling to beat the band, but Julia was looking at him so hopefully, he couldn't disappoint her.

"I'm sure it'll be just fine," he said. Julia smiled and rolled onto her side.

Jake sat down at the kitchen table with a bowl of cold soup, his sister's bread and a dish of berries. He was going to have to eat the whole pot of the blamed stuff to fill up. But he would admit it was good. Jake dunked his bread and sopped up the bottom of the bowl and cleaned his dish of strawberries. He wasn't full, but he didn't care. The sight of Julia had made his mind wander from the hunger in his stomach to a far greater hunger situated below his belt buckle. He could hardly wake her up, her looking so tired and all, but he could sit at the table and envision those legs sticking out of a thigh-length chemise. Jake closed up the house and headed to bed. If nothing else he could hold her. Jake crept into his bedroom.

"Did you like the soup?" Julia asked.

"Never heard of eating soup cold, but it was good. I figured you'd be sound asleep by now."

"I'm tired, but I was waiting for you," she said.

Jake pulled his pants down and smiled. "Were you?" Julia nodded. He climbed into bed and pulled her close. "I thought you'd be tired."

"I am," Julia said as she stroked the side of his face. "But I don't suppose it'll take longer than last night, though."

Jake didn't know whether to be insulted or thrilled. He settled for being happy as hell his wife was inching her foot up his leg. "I think I might be able to stretch things out for you, Mrs. Shelling."

"Whatever suits you, Mr. Shelling, is fine with me," she said.

Chapter Eight

JULIA AWOKE THE NEXT MORNING just as the sunlight began to filter in the window. Jake was dressing and a rooster was crowing outside. She lay still watching him run a hand through his hair.

"You don't have to get up quite yet," he said.

Julia sat up, stretched and yawned. "Yes, I do. Flossie and Harry will be here soon. They're taking me to town." Julia dropped her head, unsure of how to ask her husband for money. "Jake, I need to have some clothes more suited for here on the farm. I can cut my dresses down, but it seems a shame . . ."

"Buy whatever you want, Julia. I have a charge at Snelling's store," he said.

Julia took a clean chemise out of a drawer and pulled the one she had slept in over her head. She stretched up, reached through the lace straps and shimmied her fresh under clothes down her body. She realized then her husband was watching her.

"Buy every bolt they have as long as you promise me to get some more like that thing you're putting on," Jake said.

Julia giggled. "I have twenty or more of these, Jake in every color. How silly you are. I need to make some plain skirts and blouses." Julia picked out a dress with lavender flowers. She had a felt hat and green shoes that matched.

"Get whatever you need, Julia. I imagine you'll want to get some things for the house, too. Cramer's sells furniture and rugs and such. Millie Taylor has a dress shop in town. Maybe she'll have some ready-made things you'd like." Jake put his hat on his head. "Get whatever you want. I'll stop by and pay them next week."

"I can pick whatever I want for the house?" Julia asked with a smile.

Jake kissed her nose. "Whatever you want."

* * *

Julia bought blouses at Millie Taylor's. Fabric for skirts at Snelling's as well as melting chocolate and bright yellow material for curtains and a deep red and tan check for tablecloths. Old Mrs. Snelling had smiled smugly when she saw Julia. Julia pulled her list from her bag, and soon Jacob Snelling and his mother had to hurry to keep up with her demands. By the time she had ordered everything she needed, the Snellings and Inga were tripping over each other to pile her items on the worn wooden counter. She nearly filled Harry's wagon at Cramer's. Three colors of paint, flowered wallpaper, lamps and a round braided rug in gold and browns. Mr. Cramer was tallying up her order when Flossie came in the store.

"About ready, Julia? Harry's itching to get home," Flossie said.

Julia pulled on her lace gloves and turned to Flossie. "Oh, yes. I'm nearly finished." She turned to the balding, rotund man behind the counter. "Thank you so much, Mr. Cramer, for all your help. And you think the chandelier will be here in few weeks?"

Morton Cramer was smiling and nodding. "Yes, yes, Mrs. Shelling. In fact when it gets here I'll have my boy deliver it. Anything else you need, you just ask."

Julia stood with Flossie on the sidewalk in front of Cramer's watching Harry try to squeeze all of Julia's purchases into his wagon. "Everyone was so nice. Even Old Mrs. Snelling."

"Probably cause Jake never spent more than two nickels at a time in town," Flossie said.

"Do you think he'll be angry?" Julia asked. "He told me this morning to buy anything I wanted."

"I don't imagine for long, if he is," Flossie replied.

Julia climbed up on the wagon seat after Flossie. "He did tell me to get anything I wanted or needed. And his house, well, it needs quite a bit of work."

"Jake told you told get anything you need?" Harry asked. "Even at Cramer's?"

Julia plopped her hands in her lap and smiled as she tilted her head to the sun. "That's what he said."

* * *

Jake came in from checking the south fields near four o'clock. He had trouble all day concentrating on the problems Slim was talking about. They needed rain soon to save some of the fields on higher ground. A bug of some kind was making headway into the stored corn for the pigs and cows. Two of the hands had run off leaving Jake mighty short-handed with harvest coming soon. But he found himself nearly running to get to the house when he and Slim pulled into the yard. Jake flew into the house, grabbed Julia from behind, swung her around and kissed her.

"You're a sight for sore eyes," he said.

Julia laughed. "Hardly with my hair pulled up and paint on my nose."

Jake leaned back to look at Julia and then glanced around the living room. There were open buckets of paint and packages still tied with string. "What are you doing?"

Julia giggled. "Why painting, silly. What do you think?"

There was junk everywhere, and Jake didn't smell anything cooking. He should have been mad but Julia was grinning ear to ear. "I see you got some things from Snelling's store."

Julia whirled around from item to item, showing her purchases to Jake and explaining her plans. "I know I should have put everything away first, but I couldn't help myself. I just had to get started right away. I'm so excited I couldn't wait."

Jake chuckled. "I've never been excited about painting."

Julia picked up her brush and itched her nose with the back of her hand. "Well, I've never done it before, and I think I'm going to like it. I'm only painting the trim around the windows. I'm going to wallpaper everywhere else."

Jake turned around the room slowly. "Mother said she was going to wallpaper this room. I never got around to it after she died."

"We're going to have to order some furniture when I'm done, Jake. There's hardly anything to sit on but these old chairs." Julia studied the room. "And I think I want tall cupboards on both sides of the fireplace to hold pictures and books. What do you think?"

Jake watched her, hands on his hips. He didn't know the first thing about decorations and such. "You do what ever you want, Julia."

Julia ran to her husband and threw herself into his arms.

"Oh, Jake. Do you mean it? Anything I want? Flossie thought you might be mad I spent so much money, but there's a lot to do." She looked up at Jake. "I want to make your house a home. Where our children will grow up. Where Danny and Millie want to come and visit. Where we can sit in the evening and talk or read."

The vision Julia painted slammed into Jake and broad-sided him. A roaring fire, children playing, his wife sewing and he lounging in a chair proud as punch of his family. It was far and away more than he'd envisioned for he and Inga. He pulled Julia close in his arms.

"I'm not mad. Flossie and Gloria have been after me for ages to do something with the homestead. I'll admit I didn't know the first thing about it. And I'm sure you do. Did you get yourself something to wear, too?" he asked.

Julia looked down at herself. "This thing is stained beyond repair. I'm going to make it my work dress. I got fabric for skirts and ready-made blouses at Mrs. Taylor's. I had the most marvelous day." Jake's stomach growled. "And don't you worry about dinner. You go on out and do what ever it is you do, and I'll have dinner on the table at six."

Six was later than Jake was accustomed to eating, but Julia seemed so pleased with herself, he didn't say a word. "I don't smell anything cooking. What are we having?"

"Mrs. Snelling had jarred mayonnaise for sale. I guess that's quite a treat out here. I bought a jar and made egg salad. We'll have sandwiches and soup for dinner. I bought a chicken, too, for Sunday dinner." Julia cocked her head. "I don't really know what to do with it, though." She looked up at Jake wide-eyed. "It still has the feathers on it."

Jake laughed and kissed her forehead. "I'll clean it for you."

"Oh, thank you, Jake." Julia kissed his cheek and picked up her paintbrush. "Now you run along. I have lots to do."

He had been summarily dismissed. His wife was busy painting, and he had to pluck a chicken. Jake didn't care. When Julia smiled it lit up the room. Lit up his life. If fussing and papering made her happy, by God he'd see she could do it everyday. Julia was dabbing paint around the windows and humming. Jake headed for the bunkhouse. Cook'd be serving up stew about now.

* * *

Julia worked everyday on the sitting room. She wandered around the rest of the house, imagining the colors she would use to brighten them. In the evening, she made intricate lace table scarves for Flossie and Gloria. If it hadn't been for her sisters-in-law, she and Jake wouldn't have had bread. Jake worked on his books or read as she sewed. Last night, Jake had helped her unroll the rug. The cream and white and green flowered paper looked beautiful on the walls. The dark green and tan braided rug matched perfectly. Julia sat pictures on the mantel and found a box of things that must have been Jake's parents in a cupboard. She placed pewter candlesticks and a pipe that must have belonged to Jake's father on the mantle.

Julia heard Jake come in the house. She had browned butter and fried the trout Danny had caught and brought to her. Julia loved when Flossie brought her children with her to visit. Millie followed her around like a puppy. They had practiced walking correctly with books balanced on their heads and had ended up on the floor giggling. Julia sighed. Life was near perfect. Jake came in behind her and wrapped his arms about her waist.

"Umm," she sighed as she snuggled back against his chest. "I made fudge for dessert."

Jake worked his nose through Julia's hair. "I was thinking about something else after dinner."

Julia giggled. That part of her marriage *was* perfect. Jake told her she was the most beautiful woman on the face of the earth. When he touched her and his eyes darkened as she imagined they were now, Julia believed it was possible. They made love every night, even when Julia thought she was too exhausted to move. Every time he touched her, she was convinced their loving could not get better. But it did. She was oddly not shy around him, and Jake seemed to enjoy that the most. She knew he watched her every morning pull on her stockings and every night unbind her hair. Even naked, Julia felt perfectly at ease. Occasionally, she would hear her mother's voice in her head, chiding her for her lewd behavior. It grew increasing easier to ignore.

"Mr. Shelling, really. We haven't even eaten." Jake was whispering a bawdy comment in her ear when she heard a knock at the door. "I wonder who that is. And at the front door yet. I don't think I've ever opened your front door."

"Our front door, Julia. And I still can't believe you painted it red, inside and out," he said with a laugh.

"Oh shush. It'll look beautiful when I get the hallway and the outside of the house painted white." Julia pulled away from Jake, straightened her hair and went to answer the second knock.

The man standing there wore a checked suit and a bowler hat. Julia didn't recognize him. But a sense of dread filled her.

"Hello. May I help you?"

"Julia Crawford?" the man asked.

Julia's palms had begun to sweat and she swallowed. "Yes."

The man swept his hat off of his head. "May I come in?"

Jake pulled the door open further. "Who is it, Julia?"

Julia's perfect little life may well be crashing down around her ears in the next second. Her voice quivered as she answered her husband. "I don't know."

"Can I help you?" Jake asked.

"I'm here to see Miss Crawford. These papers will testify to my legitimacy. I need to speak to her alone," the man said to Jake as he held out an envelope.

Jake put his arm around Julia.

"Miss Crawford is now Mrs. Jake Shelling. My wife. Whatever concerns her concerns me." Julia grabbed his hand, and he squeezed it hard.

The man looked from one to the other. "May I come in?"

"We're getting ready to have supper. Can only give you a few minutes." Jake stepped aside with Julia under his arm. He pointed to the horsehair chair in front of the fireplace and seated Julia in the other. Jake stood behind her with his hand on her shoulder.

"What's your name and what's this all about?" he asked.

"Frank Smith. I'm a representative of Miss Crawford's father." The man sat back. "William Crawford."

"Her name is Mrs. Shelling," Jake said.

The man's head tilted. "From what I heard in town, her name was nearly Mrs. Jacob Snelling."

Frank Smith would report that entire humiliating experience to her parents. He was staring at Jake. "You're mistaken, sir," Julia said.

Jake squeezed her shoulders. "There was a mix-up at the station when my wife arrived. I'm thankful it happened."

The man smiled thinly. He leaned forward and began to unfold the papers in his hands. "I'm sure you recognize your father's signature."

Julia accepted the papers with shaking hands and saw her father's name boldly etched. "Yes. That is my father's signature."

Frank Smith clapped his hands together lightly and smiled. "There is good news, Miss Crawford. Your family is willing to accept you back." He sat back, "With some conditions of course."

Julia touched her hand to Jake's hand resting on her shoulder. "I don't want to go back."

"Don't be too hasty, Miss Crawford. Let me tell you what's in these papers," the man said.

"Her name is Mrs. Shelling. One more time wrong, and you'll be out on your ear," Jake replied.

Jake had not raised his voice, but the threat was clearly received by Mr. Smith. He addressed Julia as he handed her the papers. "Your inheritance will be intact, and family members will not be apprised of this unfortunate incident as long as you sign this final page."

Julia swallowed and took the paper. She read till the last line. *Her promise to respect her family's wishes. No more inappropriate or offensive behavior.* A lifetime spent with a bowed head and a broken heart as well. Tears blurred her eyes. Even with her past she'd never been so humiliated in all of her life. She was certain Jake was coming to like and respect her. She was worried she might love him.

"I don't want to go," Julia said and looked up at Jake in her misery.

Jake crouched down beside her and smiled. "Then don't."

"A half a million dollars seems worth it to me," Mr. Smith said.

Jake drew in a breath and glanced from Smith to Julia. "You're inheritance is a half a million dollars?"

Julia nodded, eyes downcast. "Please don't make me go."

"I'm sure the Crawford family would take into consideration anything you could do to make her see reason," Smith said and stared hard at Jake.

Jake tilted Julia's chin up and stared at her when he spoke to Smith. "I've got plenty of money. More than we'll ever need. We don't need her money." He turned to fix a glare on Smith. "You go back and tell her family to stick their money. I'm not up for sale and neither is she."

Julia's shoulders shook and fat tears wandered down her cheeks. She had been scared to death of Jake's reaction when he heard the amount of her inheritance. Her lip trembled. "Are there any personal notes with those papers?"

Smith snorted. "No."

"You go back and tell your employer to mind his own business. She's my wife. Tell them the marriage has been consummated, and no court in the land will interfere. Get out of our house, and don't come back. Ever," Jake said.

Smith rose slowly. Jake towered over him. He leaned in close to Jake. "Maybe you need to take some time to think on this. No telling how a man of Mr. Crawford's stature could help a dirt-hoer in South Dakota. Maybe even a nice desk job with . . ."

Jake picked Smith up by his stiff white collar. The man's face reddened, and Jake smiled. "Smart men don't question my integrity. I see you're none too smart." Jake carried Smith to the door, opened it with his free hand and tossed him outside. "Just see Mr. Crawford gets my message and my meaning." He slammed the door with a flourish and cursed a blue streak.

Julia had crumpled to the floor in a heap. Jake knelt beside her and pulled her into his lap. Pushing the hair from her face and kissing her.

"I'm sorry," Julia said between sobs. "I'm so sorry."

"Sorry about what?" he asked.

"It's a lot of money to turn down, Jake. I'm sure my father would be generous. You could buy more land or give some to Flossie and Gloria. I'm so sorry."

"Julia, listen to me. I don't want your father's money. I don't need it. You're my wife," Jake said.

"But . . ." Julia began.

"No buts about it. As long as you're sure you want to be here, I want you to stay," Jake said and kissed her forehead.

Tears poured from her eyes. "I want to stay, Jake. You're sure you want me to stay?"

Jake pulled Julia's head under his chin and rested his head on it. "I want you to stay, Julia." Julia's breathing slowed and her cries wound down as he stroked her arms.

"What man wouldn't want all these gee-gaws let alone a red front door? I don't think I could live happy without those little table cozies you make." He pulled her away to look her in the eyes and smiled softly as he did. "I'm even starting to like those teeny little sandwiches you make and cold soup, honey."

Julia started crying all over again. She knew he was trying to make her laugh, and now she was hanging on his shirt and crying.

"What? What did I say?" he asked.

Julia's lip trembled through a smile. "You called me honey. And I know you're just trying to make me feel better. And I know you eat your dinner at the bunkhouse most nights. I'm not the wife you wanted. I still don't know anything about life on the farm. I just spend your money and paint."

Jake touched his hand on her chin. "You've brought life and light into this old house, Julia. I didn't know how badly I needed it till I thought you might want to go back with Smith. You're gracious and stylish and spread that to everything you touch. I'd miss it if you left. I'm hoping one of these days we'll have a child, cause I think you'll raise smart, handsome children with manners and breeding."

"Oh, Jake, do you really think I'd be a good mother?" she asked. Could she have loved him anymore than at this moment, she wondered?

"How could you think otherwise? Do you think I'll be a good father?" he asked.

Julia smiled. "Wonderful. Unless of course we have daughters. And there's a good chance with as many sisters as you and I both have."

"If we have girls and they're as beautiful as their mother, I'll lock them in a closet till they're forty," he said.

Julia sighed and leaned into her husband's arms. Jake defended her to Frank Smith, called her honey and told her she'd make a good mother. What had started out horribly ended up more than she could have ever hoped. She was aching for his touch the full length of her body.

"Let's go upstairs, Mr. Shelling. I believe I need to lie down," she said.

"Whatever you think is best, Mrs. Shelling." Jake was smiling as he carried Julia up the steps.

Chapter Nine

J ULIA WAS PLEASED AND A little amazed at the things she'd been able to accomplish in Jake's house. They very rarely had bread, dinner was a haphazard affair, but the house was shaping up to be every bit as comfortable and inviting as she could have imagined. Jake seemed content and happy with all the things she had done. He took a tour of the house every evening when he came home and commented on each little thing. They were at the kitchen table eating crackers and canned sardines when Harry came riding into the yard. Jake jumped up when he saw his brother-in-law jump down from his horse.

"What is it?" Jake shouted to Harry.

"Gloria. It's time. Flossie wants Julia to help," Harry said.

"Oh dear," Julia said. She turned and hurried back into the house. She was back on the porch in minutes with a bundle in her arms.

"What's that?" he asked.

"Flossie told me to pack rags, sheets and nightgowns when Gloria's time came. There'd be less wash then in case we didn't have time. Hurry, Jake, get the wagon," Julia said and pulled on his sleeve.

Slim had the wagon hitched in no time, and they bounced off as fast as Jake could force the horses. It seemed like forever to Julia.

"I wonder if Will went for the doctor?" Jake asked.

"I imagine so, Jake," she said.

Julia jumped down from the wagon herself and hurried into the house, Jake trailing her. "Flossie, how are things? Did Will go for the doctor? What can I do?" she asked.

"The doctor's out at the Wilson place. One of the boys nearly lost a foot in an accident. It's you and me for now, Julia," Flossie said.

Julia hurried past a pacing white-faced Will and into the bedroom where Gloria lay. She laid her hand on Gloria's sweat-sheened forehead. "How are you doing, Gloria? Do you need anything?"

Gloria grimaced. "I wish this baby would hurry up and get here."

Flossie didn't turn from tearing old sheets in two. "I told you. Babies come when babies come. Nothing we can do to hurry them."

Julia rinsed a rag in water and wiped Gloria's face. "Take deep breaths, Gloria."

Flossie looked at Julia. "You're not squeamish are you?"

Julia shook her head. "No. What needs to be done?"

"Get the water boiled. And stir the potatoes. I have a feeling we're going to be here for awhile."

Julia went to the kitchen with Millie trailing behind.

"Aunt Julia?" Millie said.

There were tears in the little girl's eyes. Julia picked her up. "What is it Millie?"

"Is Aunt Gloria gonna die? Danny said Billy Owen's ma died when she had his brother," Millie asked.

Julia kissed Millie's nose. "No. Your Aunt Gloria is strong. Sometimes first babies take a while. We're going to brew some tea to make it easier for her. Do you want to help?"

Millie nodded and shimmied down Julia's side. They boiled water for the doctor, brewed tea and checked the dinner Flossie had started. Julia was beginning to worry as the evening dragged on. By the middle of the night, Julia was sick to her stomach with fear. Even Flossie looked worried. The kids had fallen asleep in Harry's lap, when Jake read a story long ago. Will sat slumped against the wall in the corner. Harry and Jake watched Flossie and Julia enter the bedroom and exit.

"I just don't know what's the matter," Flossie whispered after closing the door on the men in the sitting room. "This baby's ready to come."

Julia looked at her watch, pinned to her blouse. It was near four in the morning. She pulled the sheet up, exposing Gloria's protruding stomach. "I think the baby's turned a funny way, Flossie. Feel." Julia guided Flossie's hand. "See? It feels like the head is on the side here."

Flossie skimmed her hand over her sister's stomach. "My kids were born quick. With no trouble. I wish that doctor would get here."

Julia looked at Flossie and leaned close to a moaning and thrashing Gloria. "I'm going to try and help move the baby around, Gloria. It's going to hurt."

"I don't think she can hear what we're saying anymore. Go on do something if you think you could help," Flossie said.

Her sister-in-law was worried to death. Julia could see it in her eyes. Usually happy eyes, Julia thought. Funny how she never noticed Flossie's scar much anymore. Would Flossie wonder where she had come upon this knowledge of child bearing?

"It's going to hurt her. Hold her down," Julia said.

Julia massaged and kneaded Gloria's stomach till her hands were weak and cramped. It felt as though she was making progress though. "Get behind her shoulders, Flossie. She has to push while I move this child."

Flossie spoke gently till she realized Gloria was near passed out. She began to shout as if Gloria were a small child caught in an errant act. "You wake up this instant, Gloria Jean Shelling. I mean it. You got to get awake and push. Come on, Gloria."

Gloria moaned and Flossie and Julia screamed and begged for every bit of strength she had left. "The baby's crowning, Flossie. Come on Gloria. Push." The door flew open just as Julia saw the top of the baby's head.

Will passed out into Harry and Jake's arms as a weary Doctor Hammish pushed by. "What's going on here? Get that fool husband out of here. Where we at, Flossie?"

"Thank God you're here," Flossie said. "The baby wouldn't come, Doc. Julia pushed on Gloria's stomach. I think she got the head going the right way cause she's crowning."

Doctor Hammish examined Gloria and looked up at Julia and Flossie. "This baby needs born right now, and Gloria's got to dig deep and do the work. She looks near exhaustion. Get her pushing, girls."

Flossie and Julia held Gloria's shoulders and splashed cold water on her face. "It's time, Gloria. Start pushing again," Flossie yelled.

Tears ran down Gloria's face and every push brought an agony of pain to her face. But near five in the morning, a small healthy boy finally was born.

Flossie was holding the baby, crying and crooning and swaying back and forth. Doctor Hammish looked at Julia while he finished with a passed out Gloria. "Mighty glad you moved that child around. He'd been dead before long. You a nurse?"

"No," Julia said. She bent down to pick up bloody sheets.

"How did you know what to do?" Flossie asked.

Julia wiped tears of joy and remembrance from her cheeks. "I was with my mother when she had my youngest sister. She had a similar trouble. I was glad I could help."

Gloria stirred, and Flossie handed the baby to Julia and hurried to her sister's side. "Take him out so his father and uncles can see him. They're worried sick."

Julia held the warm bundle in her arms. He was so small. So beautiful. So very precious. She walked slowly to the sitting room. "Your son wants to say hello, Will."

Gloria's husband jumped from the floor with a tear-stained face. His hands trembled as he took his son into his arms. He looked at Julia, lips quivering. "Gloria?"

"Doctor Hammish says she's going to be fine." Harry shook his head and wiped his mouth. Jake stood and went out the door. Will's eyes closed, and he mouthed what Julia figured was a prayer of thanksgiving. "She's going to need complete bed rest. I'm going to get some sleep. Flossie will stay till I get back."

Will dropped into a chair and rocked his son back and forth. Julia went outside. She needed fresh air and her husband's arms. He was kneeling beside an oak tree, his hand steadied on the rough bark, his head dropped and shoulders shaking. Julia laid her hand on his shoulder. He had been her strength too many times already. She would be his if she could.

"Jake?" she said.

Jake shook his head and swiped at tears. He sniffed and cleared his throat. "If anything would have happened to Gloria, I don't know what I would have done." He stared at Julia. "For whatever you and Flossie did, I thank you."

Julia smiled and yawned. "I was worried, too, but everyone's going to be fine. You need to get me home so I can get some sleep. Flossie's going to stay till I get back."

* * *

Jake ducked into the house and went straight to Gloria's bed. He kissed his youngest sister's forehead and looked at Flossie holding her hand. Will sat on the edge of the bed.

"I'm going to take Julia home. We'll be back. Let me see my new nephew." Will gingerly handed Jake the bundle. Jake pulled back the blanket. Ten little fingers, a strong chin and a head full of dark hair like Gloria's. Jake's mouth quivered, and all he could do was nod as he lay the baby down beside his mother. Flossie grabbed Jake's hand.

"Thank God Julia was here. I didn't know what to do. Doc says she saved Gloria and Joshua both. Take good care of your wife, Jake. She doesn't look it, but she's got a backbone made for life on a farm," Flossie said.

Jake pulled up to his house as the sun rose. Julia was long asleep against his shoulder. He was so damned proud of his wife. And thankful as well. His little round, soft, weak wife had saved his sister. She wasn't really weak, Jake knew. The bloody sheets she had lugged had made bile rise in his throat. And he had heard her through the door shouting at his sister like a cattle drover at a passel of mules. He was thinking she brought him a whole lot more than pretty things and comfort when she married him. He was never so glad Portentia Snelling's feet were arthritic. He'd have to buy the old bag some little gift in thanks.

* * *

The week went by with more on the dinner table than usual. Julia spent most of days at Gloria and Will's helping out and with Flossie there cooking more times than not, Julia usually climbed up into his wagon holding a dish filled with his sister's cooking. Julia's household projects had gone by the wayside as well as her smile. She talked enthusiastically about her new nephew and Millie and Danny and then would fall silent and staring at the landscape on their ride home. She seemed distant and a little sad. Maybe she was pining over starting a family of their own.

"What's the matter?" Jake asked Julia as he ate some of the stew Flossie had sent that day, over a week since Joshua was born.

Julia's head came up as if far away in her thoughts. "Oh, nothing," she said.

Jake eyed his wife. Her normal happy chatter was still non-existent. "You've been awful quiet lately. Something bothering you?" he asked.

Julia picked up her spoon and began to eat. "No. Nothing's bothering me."

Jake continued to study her while he ate. He had problems of his own. Three more hands had quit, and Slim said there were no men to hire in town. Every farm for miles had a full contingent of workers and even higher wages weren't inducing men to change bosses right before harvest. Will and Harry said they'd help as much as they could, but they each had farms of their own. And with Will and Gloria's new baby, Jake doubted Will could give him more than a few hours a week.

"Going to be tough harvest," Jake said.

"Why's that?" Julia asked absently.

"Not enough men. Nobody to hire either. Cook's going to have to work with me. Flossie said she'd come over to help you," Jake said and tore bread from the loaf.

"Help me what?" Julia asked.

It didn't always register in Jake's head that Julia would not understand. She'd grown up a pampered daughter, not a farm child. Maybe after harvest he'd plan a late honeymoon in Sioux Falls. A change of scenery may be all Julia needed. "There's going to be seven men to cook for, not counting me and you. Breakfast and supper as well."

"Oh dear."

"Flossie will help. Make lots of beans and biscuits," Jake said.

Julia nodded blankly.

"And plenty of meat. We'll be tired, everyone of us and hungry as bears in the spring," Jake added.

"Why don't we have enough men?" Julia asked.

"Don't know. Never had this problem before." He shrugged his shoulders. "Just bad luck this year I suppose." Jake turned to a knock at the door. "Come on in, Slim."

"Jake's sister sent stew, Slim. Would you like some?" Julia asked.

"No Ma'am. Kind of you to offer." The wizened man turned to Jake. "We got problems, boss."

"What now?"

Slim turned his hat in his hand. "Two more boys done and quit on us. Phelps and Withrow. Don't know how we're going to bring this corn in."

Jake jumped from his chair. "What?"

"Two more boys, boss. And the part I don't like is that some dandy gave 'em two hundred dollars to do it," Slim repeated.

Jake sat down slowly in his chair. "What are you talking about?"

"Well, I don got suspicious when the others quit. Rode into town with Phelps, Saturday night. We was a playing cards when he, Phelps that is, up and left the table. I laid down two pair to follow 'em," Slim said.

"Why'd you get suspicious?" Jake asked.

"Just didn't seem right somehow when Jethro Melton quit last week. He's been with us every harvest going on six years, and when he left, he done rode out with out even a goodbye," Slim said.

"Where did Mr. Phelps go when he left the poker table, Slim?" Julia asked.

"That's the thing. He was standing outside the saloon jawing with some city man. When he sees me, he stuffs a whole wad of bills in his pocket and takes off. I knew that boy's family for years. Didn't seem right him acting so strange with such an upright Ma and Pa. So's I hightail it on outa town till I catches him." Slim dropped his head. "Said some man gave him two hundred dollars not to work for you."

"Why in God's name would someone chase off my hands. And who would be fool enough to spend that kind of money to do it?" Jake asked. Julia looked ghost pale when he turned to her.

"What did the man look like, Slim? The one that gave Mr. Phelps the money," Julia asked.

Slim scratched his head. "That's the funny part of all this. Never saw him before. He weren't from around here that's for sure. Some fancy checked suit and one of them round hats. What they called?" Slim asked.

"Bowler hats," Julia answered.

"What are you getting at, Julia?" Jake asked as he turned his attention from his foreman to his wife. "What's the difference what kind of hat the man wore?"

Julia's eyes darted. "Mr. Smith wore a bowler hat, Jake," she whispered.

"Who?" Recognition dawned on Jake. "Why in the hell would Smith . . ." He fell silent and stared at his wife. "What are you thinking?"

"I'm thinking Mr. Smith was instructed by my father to do anything to make you see reason," Julia said.

"Your father doesn't own me, Julia," Jake said, shaking with anger. "What in God's name does he hope to accomplish by running my hands away at harvest?"

"Going to put us in a bad way, boss," Slim said. "If'n that what the man set out to do, he did it."

"Thanks, Slim," Jake said as he slowly turned around in his seat. The bang of the screen door made him jump with a start. Julia's head was bowed, and tears trickled down her face. What in the hell kind of family did she come from? Jake reached for her hand, and she pulled away. He stood, picked her up out of her chair and sat his wife in his lap. He kissed her hair when she turned her face away from him.

"Your father's not going to change my mind, Julia. You're staying. You're my wife. For better or worse," he said in a low voice.

"I didn't hear all my vows at the train station that day, Jake. It was too loud." Julia sniffed. "This certainly would qualify though as worse."

Jake chuckled softly and rubbed his nose in her hair. "I own this property free and clear. Have a small mortgage on some equipment I bought last year, and I was hoping to pay it off from the harvest this fall. If we can't get the crops in, then we'll pay it next year. Might have to cut back a bit, though."

Julia shook her head against Jake's chest. "I won't buy anymore paint."

"I think we can afford paint, but the furniture you were planning on buying might have to wait. I'm sorry."

Julia sat up straight on Jake's lap. "You're sorry. I'm the one that got you into this mess in the first place."

Jake turned her to face him. "I don't understand what your father's trying to accomplish. You're a married woman with or without his consent. Running off my help won't change that."

Julia lowered her lashes. "Father may have not told Smith to ruin you, but I don't imagine he questioned his methods." Julia looked Jake square in the eye. "Father and Mother won't be able to stand the thought that I've done something so stupid as to run off and get married. What will they say to their friends? If they get me back under their roof, well . . ."

Jake placed his hands on Julia's cheeks and lifted her face till she looked at him. "Listen to me, Julia Shelling. I don't care what a bunch of society people think. We're a thousand miles away. Just tell your parents to forget about it. The only people we have to worry about is us."

"Make love to me, Jake," Julia said.

Jake held her face in his hands. Every fear, hope and dream was visible there. Their lovemaking was reassuring to her. It was a hell of a lot more than that to him. More than a man's release, a symptom of him being born male. It offered more than physical comfort to him. This beautiful woman wanted him, needed him in a way no one else did. When Julia curled up to him, responded to him, he felt as if he was the biggest, smartest man God had ever graced the earth with. After years of wondering if he'd done the best by his family, by the legacy his parents left him, when Julia touched his chest as she was doing now, Jake was convinced he'd succeed against any obstacle. Was this love? Was this what Flossie was trying to tell him?

"I'd be happy to oblige you, Mrs. Shelling," he said.

Jake carried her to their bedroom. Their clothes slipped to the floor in a heap until they both stood naked before each other.

"You are too beautiful to grace my bed, Julia," Jake said as his eyes swept her head to toe.

Julia smiled softly and ran her hands up his wide arms. "I never thought in a hundred years I'd be married to a man as handsome and kind as you."

Jake kissed her deeply and she inched up to him, her breasts touching his chest. He tilted her head back in his hands. "Don't ever leave me, Julia," he said.

"Why would I want to leave you, Jake?" Julia whispered against his mouth. "You make me forget I'm silly and clumsy and fat."

Jake watched his hand run down the side of her breast and follow the curve of her waist and hip. "Don't say that, Julia." He stared into her eyes. "There isn't an ounce of flesh on you I want to part with."

Julia's eyes fluttered when he spoke, and he inched her to the bed, gently easing himself down on top of her. Her legs spread under him, and he slipped inside her body. That moment when they joined always made Jake draw a sharp breath. As if he'd been searching for water in a desert and had been suddenly drenched in a cool rain. As if he'd been looking all his life for the place, the spot he'd fit in this world and found it each time his wife drew him in.

* * *

Julia cherished their lovemaking. She needed Jake, needed this more than chocolate, more than a home free of ridicule. She opened her eyes to look at him. Was this what she had been searching for? This magical rhythm when he moved in her. Being for those moments pressed under him the most attractive woman in the world. Julia lifted her hips up to meet his thrusts. Gratification was whirling down around her, surrounding her, forcing her breath to come in pants.

"No need to try and stretch this out, Mr.Shelling," she said. As often as Jake promised hours of endless pleasure in Julia's ear, he rarely succeeded. She didn't mind.

"Whatever makes you happy, Mrs. Shelling," Jake groaned and arched into her one final time. Jake rolled on his back bringing Julia atop of him.

"God, woman. I swear you make me see stars," he said.

Julia laid her head down on Jake's chest. "Jake?" she whispered.

"Hmm," he sighed as he stroked her back.

"Will we be able to do it? Bring the crops in?" Julia lifted her head. "Will I be able to feed you all?"

He touched her chin with his finger. "With you beside me, Julia, we can do anything."

Chapter Ten

FALL WAS COMING AS THE nights grew cooler and leaves began their change from green to gold and the anticipation of unrelenting work. Julia rode to Flossie's or Gloria's in the wagon, and they taught her the basics of feeding a kitchen full of hungry men. But her biscuits didn't always rise, and sometimes her bread baked flatter than when it went in the oven. She made fudge at Flossie's and showed Millie how to make paper dolls. The day finally came when Jake and Slim decided it was time to bring in the corn. The next morning Jake and Julia were up before sunrise. Julia made omelets the first morning. She would not do that again. She had made twelve of them before men stopped raising empty plates. Julia ate toast. It was all that was left. Scrambled eggs and ham would do fine the next day.

Julia was watching what she ate, anyway. Miraculously, her skirts seemed too big for her. She moved buttons over on every one, and she had no intentions of having to move them back. Flossie floured and roasted the biggest piece of meat Julia had ever seen. She and Millie decided they hated the feel of raw meat and let Flossie fit it in to a pan Julia was sure she would never be able to lift. Julia, Danny and Millie painted silly faces on the wall in the kitchen.

"Mine has buck teeth like Jimmy Wilkins, Aunt Julia," Danny said.

Millie swiped her nose and left a trail of bright yellow paint. "My tree doesn't look much like a tree."

"Don't worry," Julia said. "After harvest I'm going to paint all the walls. I'll cover it up. But for now we can pretend we're Michelangelo."

"Michael who?" Danny asked.

"He was an Italian painter and sculptor," Julia replied.

"What are you three up to?" Flossie asked from her spot at the kitchen sink.

Julia looked at her niece and nephew and giggled. "We're practicing to be famous painters."

Flossie turned and eyed the work. "I don't know how famous any of you are going to be. Come on now, Millie, and get the table set. Danny, go see to your Uncle's horses. I hear the men coming."

Julia jumped up and turned her head to see Flossie's watch. "Is it that late already?"

"Four o'clock. Men'll be ready to eat."

* * *

After the men ate, Julia insisted Flossie go home to Harry. Julia washed dishes till her hands were raw. Julia hit the bed dog-tired. Jake plopped down beside her. "How many days is it going to take, Jake?"

His eyes were closed and his arm lay across his forehead. "Weeks at this pace."

The days did indeed roll into weeks. Julia was tired from a week ago piled on tired from today. The house needed dusting, and empty paint cans still sat in the hall. She'd never dreamed cooking could be so exhausting. First thing she gathered eggs and hauled milk to the kitchen. Then she cooked. Then she did dishes. Then she cooked. Then she did dishes. Jake was exhausted, too, she could tell. Some mornings he didn't bother shaving. He just didn't have time. Jake finally announced they'd be done by week's end.

"Oh, thank God," Julia said and slumped into a chair.

"We'll never get the south field in before frost, and the corn's already sat too long on the stalk. We'll get done what we can get done and call it a season," he said.

"I hate to see you give up," Julia said.

Jake rubbed the blistered calluses on his hand. "We're not giving up, Julia. We did everything we could do." He touched her hand. "All of us."

The next morning Jake was gone to the fields before she woke up. She started stew like Flossie showed her and found an old pair of Jake's pants. Julia rolled up the hem and belted them with a red silk scarf. She pulled on one of Jake's flannel shirts and an old pair of barn shoes Gloria had given her. They hadn't done everything they could do. Even though Jake said they would make it, Julia felt as though she needed to bring in the last ear of corn herself if she had to. This mess was because of her. She hurried out the door when she saw Slim taking the wagon out into the field.

"Wait, Slim. I want to help," Julia said as she climbed in beside the old man.

* * *

Jake did a double take when he saw Julia riding along side Slim. "Julia, what in God's name are you doing out here and what are you wearing?"

Julia jumped down from the wagon. "I've come to help, Jake."

Jake whoahed the horse while the men separating the corn from the stalk wiped their faces and emptied jugs of water. "My wife doesn't work in a field, Julia Shelling. You go on back to the house and get dinner ready."

"Dinner's on the stove, Jake Shelling. And you told me anything we had to do we could do as long as we were together," Julia shouted back.

The men chuckled into their sleeves. Where had his meek frightened wife gone, Jake wondered? "This isn't what I was talking about."

"Show me what to do," Julia said.

"You're going to have blisters, Julia," Jake said as he jumped from the wagon.

"As if you don't. Now quit wasting time and show me what to do," Julia said.

Jake drove Julia home in his wagon and left the rest of the men to finish the day's work late afternoon. She was clinging to the seat, he imagined, too dog-tired to sit up on her own.

"What in God's name have you been doing, Julia Shelling?" Flossie asked as she held open the back door.

"Bringing in corn," Julia said breathlessly and slid into a chair.

Flossie stirred the potatoes on the stove. "What did my brother have to say about that?"

"He wasn't too happy," Jake said as he came into the kitchen. He walked to his wife, barely in her chair and lifted her hand. "These blisters will need broken."

"I wanted to help," Julia said and accepted a cool glass of water from Millie. The liquid ran down her chin and onto the front of Jake's shirt.

"I put clean water in your room. Go wash. You'll feel better," Flossie said. She shooed Julia till she began up the steps.

"What were you thinking, Jake. Letting Julia work out there. She's no farm girl," Flossie chided.

"She wouldn't listen to me. I told her twenty times to get on home." Jake plopped down on a chair. "She feels bad 'cause she thinks this is her fault."

Flossie turned from the stove. "What's her fault?"

Jake shared Julia's suspicions. "She's convinced this Smith character's behind my losing hands."

"None of that would surprise me from what Julia's told me of her family. She's scared to death you're going to take an offer from her father and send her home to Boston." Flossie turned to face Jake. "You know that's why she jumped in your bed her first day here."

"I know. She told me." Jake slowly rose to his feet at a knock at the front door. "I wonder who that is? If it's that Smith fella, he's in for a lot worse than getting thrown out on his ass."

Jake recognized Julia's mother immediately. Similar features and exactly the same hair color. That was where the similarities ended. For every soft quality of Julia's face her mother's contrasted with a hard edge. Her father was mid-fifties, well-dressed with dark hair only slightly gray at the temples. They looked like the people on the front of the new Montgomery Wards catalog.

"May I help you?" he asked.

* * *

Julia was so bone tired; she didn't think she could move. But she was hungry, too. She lay flat back on her bed while her stomach rumbled. She'd never fall asleep like this. Julia peeled off the work boots, washed her hands and face and pulled back her knotted hair with a string. She would eat some stew with Jake and Flossie and fall into bed in an hour. At the top of the steps Julia heard Jake speaking to someone in the front hallway.

"Well, she's lying down. You can visit her tomorrow."

"Which room is hers? I'll go see her myself."

Julia sat down on the step when her knees gave out. Her mother was here.

"Why don't you at least ask these folks if they want a drink or to sit a spell?" Flossie said.

"The serving girl seems to have more sense than Julia's husband," William Crawford said.

And her father, too, now referring to Flossie as the serving girl. Julia stood straight and prepared herself. She was no longer under their control. She was Jake's wife, she chanted. Julia glided down the steps from the landing as if in a ball gown.

"Mother, Father. What a surprise."

"Good Lord, Julia. What are you wearing?" Jane Crawford asked.

William Crawford turned his ire on Jake. "You have my daughter working as a field hand?"

"I helped in the fields today. Mr. Smith paid off Jake's hands to leave in the middle of harvest," Julia said. Her insides were churning, and she felt as if she were twelve-years-old but she was determined not to let her parents see her anguish. Julia slipped her arm through Flossie's. "This is my sister-in-law. Flossie. Have you met my husband?"

"Get your things, Julia. You've caused your mother considerable worry. And change clothes, for God's sakes.

You'll not be getting on the train with us looking like a field hand," William said.

Jake started to laugh. "You people are amazing. Do you think you can waltz into my house and tell my wife to pack her things?"

"We're saving you considerable embarrassment, Mr. Shelling. And you'll certainly be compensated for your trouble," Jane Crawford said and smiled. She turned to Julia. "Come along, Julia. This nonsense has gone on long enough."

"What are you talking about? What embarrassment?" Flossie asked.

Jane Crawford looked Flossie up and down and lingered long enough on Flossie's scar to cause Flossie's cheeks to redden. "You don't know Julia as well as we do. She needs care. Needs to be looked after and kept out of trouble."

Julia was scared she was going to be sick to her stomach right there in the hallway. Her hands were shaking with embarrassment, and her face a pasty white color. "I'm doing just fine, Mother. I'm staying here."

William Crawford threw his hands up in the air. "Obviously you're not doing fine, Julia. Look at yourself."

* * *

Jake stepped in front of Flossie and Julia. He was intent on blocking the women from the poison being spilled in his own home. Julia looked as if she was going to crumble into a heap, and Flossie's hand absently went to her cheek as she did for years after her accident.

"This is my home, my property and that's my wife and sister behind me. You're Julia's parents. If she wants to speak to you, I'll allow it. But I won't allow any more of your threats. No court in the land will side with you. She's my wife. If you want to visit, fine. But no more upsetting either of them. Do you understand?"

William Crawford threw a quick glance to his wife and looked at Jake. "Why don't you and I talk alone?"

"No," Julia shouted.

One arched brow raised on Jane Crawford's face. "It certainly is well within his rights as father to get to know the man you married, Julia. I'm sure *he* has nothing to hide."

"We'll sit in the kitchen. Together," Jake said.

Flossie brewed coffee. Jane Crawford dusted her chair with a hanky before seating herself. Julia sat down across from her mother and Jake stood behind her.

"Julia's been working on the harvest with me because all of our field hands were bought off with your Mr. Smith's two hundred dollars. I don't want my wife working in the sun, sweating and toiling, but I'm damn proud to say she did it anyway."

Jake rested his hands on Julia's shoulders. "She's been aching to hear news of home, especially when Smith said he had no personal news. I imagine this is as good a time as any to get acquainted. You've met Flossie here. She's married and has two children. She lives just south of here with her husband Harry. My other sister Gloria and her husband Will had their first child about a month ago. We might have lost Gloria if not for Julia's help. Now what of Julia's sisters?"

It pained Jake to no end to be civil. These were the very people that made Julia feel obligated to shuck corn. Sanctimonious, snobby city folk that they were sitting here at his kitchen table trying to make Julia uncomfortable. But they *were* her parents, come all the way from Boston.

William and Jane Crawford stared at Jake. "This is hardly a social call," William Crawford said.

Jake's hold on Julia's shoulders tightened. "I can't imagine what else it would be."

"Mr. Snelling," Jane Crawford began.

"Shelling."

"Oh, yes, that's right. There seems to have been a mix-up at the train station," Jane replied as she stared at Julia. "From the letters Julia left, we were under the impression she was marrying a storekeeper she had corresponded with. We can't imagine what mischief she'd gotten into to marry the wrong man," Jane said as she trilled a laugh. "Your sister's found the report quite exceptional."

Julia's neck reddened, Jake saw, as he stared down at her. "Julia got into no mischief, Mrs. Crawford. The mistake was mine. Although now, I'm thankful I made the error. Now what of her sisters and her friend Eustace?"

Flossie smiled as she sat down. "And your grandson? Does he call you Nana?"

Jane Crawford stared daggers at Flossie. "William is his name. He is fine."

"Eustace is the maid," Julia's father said. "We know nothing personal about her."

* * *

"How are Jennifer and Jolene?" Julia asked.

Never had her family's coldness been more evident. Nothing in her past until her marriage had given contrast to the life she'd led. These two finely-dressed strangers were sculptures of people. Not real life honest to goodness, living, breathing humans, faults and virtues tied together. Her new family, Jake's family, meant more to her in two months than her own parents.

"Did Jillian start school?" she asked.

"She started a few weeks ago," Jane Crawford said and stared at Julia. "I believe she may be having some trouble adjusting. She says she's feeling quite abandoned."

Julia's lip began to tremble. She knew her mother had noticed. She had the look of smug self-righteousness Julia had seen so often. "No one has abandoned her. Surely it's just nerves."

"I don't know, Julia. Jillian seemed adrift when we left her in her room." Jane Crawford arched a brow. "She's never been good at making friends. Little experience with girl's her own age. But I believe this separation will do her good in the end."

Julia had tried to explain to the girl she needed a life of her own. A home of her own. But what would a ten-year-old interpret Julia's plans as other than abandonment. Jillian had begged Julia to marry a man in Boston so they would remain close. But Julia knew she needed to get far away. Away from her mother's control and the constant reminders of her own failures. Poor Jillian would be adrift and lonely at boarding school. Much like Julia herself was. Her years at school remained firmly entrenched as some of the most miserable time of her life. Tears came to Julia's eyes.

"Separation isn't enlightening for everyone, Mother. Sometimes it's sheer hell."

"Your language, Julia," her father chided. "We've raised you better than that."

Jake cleared his throat. "Maybe Julia's sister would like to spend Christmas or even next summer with us." Julia touched Jake's hand as it touched her shoulder. "We'd be happy to have her."

"Jillian Crawford has a duty to the family as do all my children. There is nothing to be learned here that will help her in that endeavor. And really, do you think I'd let her live in this, this," Jane said with a sweep of her hand, "hovel?"

"I'm only thinking of my wife's happiness. And I imagine we could keep Jillian fed and clothed will she visited. Even in this hovel," Jake said.

"We're not here to discuss Jillian. We're here to take Julia home," William Crawford said.

Julia shook her head to dismiss the heartache she was feeling for Jillian. "No. I'm not going. I'm married and happy. Go home and tell your friends whatever you will. I don't really care."

William Crawford eyed Jake and Flossie. "There are private matters we wish to discuss with our daughter. If you'd excuse us."

Flossie raised a brow at Jake and left the kitchen. "There's nothing for you to discuss that I'm not privy to. Julia's my wife. I'm staying," he said.

Jane Crawford smiled benignly. "Of course, Mr. Shelling."

"No, Jake. I'll be fine. Go on with Flossie. I'll be there in a moment."

Jake leaned down and kissed her cheek. "I'll be in the sitting room if you need me."

"How attentive your new husband is, Julia. Dare say, I'll be telling your sisters you've bewitched him with your favors."

Julia's father stared at her as Jake left the room. "You do realize Jillian will be losing her inheritance if you stay, Julia. Your mother and I will tend to her education, but she'll be no heiress," he said.

Julia fully anticipated this tactic from her parents. Her heart was racing when she replied what she only recently comprehended. "Money isn't everything, Father. Jillian is beautiful and smart. She'll need no inheritance to gain a man's favor. And certainly, I'll provide whatever assistance I can."

"Surely you won't be waiting for our will to be read, Julia," Jane Crawford said. "One never knows if a parent has had a change of heart, possibly favoring a more . . . eligible recipient."

"You would deny me my share?" Julia asked. "I've done everything my whole life for the good of the Crawford family. Until it's broken my heart. And you deem me unworthy?"

William Crawford took Julia's hand in his. "Now you know dear, Jolene feels it is highly irregular to split the family inheritance four ways. After all . . ."

Julia snatched her hand away. "I know, I know. I know all about Jolene's feelings. They've been shoved down my throat for twenty-six years. Jillian is one matter, but you would write *me* out of your will because I married and moved away? That's what you're saying, isn't it? I would think you'd be happy I'm gone. I've done nothing my whole life but embarrass you."

"Don't use that tone with us, Julia," Jane Crawford said tightly. "Any embarrassment you've caused has been of your own design. Crawfords do not run away from home. Crawfords do not disregard their family name. Crawfords do not desert their family."

Julia stood now shaking with anger. "I am no longer a Crawford. My name is Shelling. Shellings, I've found, think more about the people they love than what everyone else thinks. And I didn't run away from home. I ran away from you, Mother, and your constant belittlement. The Shelling name means more to me in two months than the Crawford name ever will." Julia looked up to see Jake standing in the doorway. She hadn't realized she'd been screaming. Julia was sure his intense gaze was the only thing keeping her on her feet.

Jane Crawford rose slowly, gathered her purse and lightly touched her husband's arm. "Come along, William." She stared at Julia. "Julia is burning bridges she may need in the future. Let her find out on her own what her folly will bring."

"Why? Why do you care Julia is married and moved?" Jake asked. "You don't want her in Boston."

"My family is my life's work, Mr. Shelling. I don't expect or accept impertinence. Especially from one as misguided as Julia." Jane Crawford tilted her head and smiled tightly. "Julia needs to remain at home. With us. She needs my guidance."

William Crawford came around the table and stood in front of Julia. "Why would you run away from your mother, Julia? She's only had your best interests at heart."

Silent tears dripped from Julia's chin. She looked up at her father. He gazed at her as if seeing a stranger.

"Oh, Father. You were at the office all the time. I don't suppose you ever knew what was said and done. But it's not your fault. It's mine. I should have left years ago." Julia dropped her head and looked back at her father's face with a plea. "Tell Jillian I love her and miss her. Will you Father? Will you tell her?"

William Crawford tilted his head. "Yes, dear, of course, I'll tell her." He cupped Julia's chin in his hand. "Are you happy, my dear?"

Julia smiled. "Yes, I'm very happy." Her father turned and followed his wife out the door.

Julia could not face Jake or Flossie. She edged past them without a word or look and ran to her room.

* * *

Jake climbed into bed with Julia that night and brushed the stray hairs from her face. She was exhausted. Dried tracks of tears marred her pale cheeks. She tossed and turned fitfully. Jake pulled her into his arms. She settled onto his shoulder with a sigh, and he held her tight, until her breathing evened and she slept peacefully. He could not.

Julia's mother was a snake in the grass. Waiting patiently for her moment to strike and impose the most damage. Jake didn't know what to make of her father. There was something going on that Jake didn't understand. An air about the two women charged as if lightning had struck them. Jake kissed Julia's forehead. She would tell him eventually, he was sure.

Jake was certain now that he loved this woman in his arms. Julia had surprised him and probably herself since their marriage. She had charmed his sisters, was beloved by his niece and nephew and would have undying devotion from Will for saving Gloria. Harry said she was just what the doctor ordered for Jake.

Julia, although clearly a woman Jake thought as he rubbed her arm, was as comfortable with Millie and Danny as she was with adults. Sometimes he felt out of his depths with his niece and nephew. Sometimes he ran out of patience with their questions. Julia encouraged the questions, the wonder, the pure vision of a child still unsullied by life's woes. She played make-believe as if a stage actress. Yet she painted walls and shucked corn as an adult with the full weight of a person who knows her place, her responsibility and accepted them. He knew she was happy here. He was happy as hell. Jake couldn't wait till Julia was pregnant. She would be a wonderful mother.

Chapter Eleven

THE NEXT MORNING, JAKE TUCKED the blankets around Julia and kissed her forehead. Her eyes fluttered open. "You stay in bed as long as you want today, Julia. I mean it," he said to her shaking head. "You had a tough day yesterday."

"You're too good to me, Jake. I'm sure Flossie never lies around in bed."

Jake chuckled and snapped his suspenders. "That's cause Millie and Danny want their breakfast. Not that Harry would care." He leaned down and kissed her lips. "You'll have children to wake you at the crack of dawn soon enough."

Julia smiled and blushed. "I hope so, Jake. I say a prayer every night that this night will be the one to give us a baby. I'm so sorry about my parents, Jake. I don't know what to say. I could have died when my mother stared at Flossie's scar."

"A sickle came loose and the blade caught her cheek when she was about fourteen." Jake took a deep breath. "She didn't look in the mirror for a full year."

"She could have been killed," Julia said.

Jake nodded. "Yes, she could have been. I thank God every day we were lucky. But a young girl with a long angry scar across her cheek struggles as well. She never thought any man would look at her. But then Harry came along and well, I don't even think he noticed, he was so head over heels in love with her."

"Harry loves Flossie. Not her face or her money or land. He loves her."

Jake sat down on the edge of the bed and picked up her hand. "There's more to love than looks that's for sure. When we first married, Julia, I was convinced you were wrong for me. That I could never love you." He touched her cheek softly. "You're the most beautiful woman I've ever seen, Julia Shelling. But that doesn't have a damn thing to do with me loving you. I love you in spite of your pretty face, not because of it."

Tears rolled from Julia's eyes. "I love you so much, Jake. I can hardly tell you how much. I was so scared my first few weeks here. But when you said that night in the kitchen that my family had been wrong about Turner. That I wasn't to blame. I think I knew then I would love you for the rest of my life."

Jake raised her hand to his lips. To his shock he realized his hands were shaking. Admitting you loved someone was harder business than he'd expected. He had held his breath till Julia said she loved him. Jake knew then he'd move heaven and earth to make her happy. He stroked the side of her face.

"Your mother and you seem to be at odds about something, Julia. Something more than just you moving here." Julia turned away and stared out the window. "Don't say anything you're not ready to. We'll be together forever, Julia."

"What if you don't always love me? What if you change your mind? I don't think I could stand it, Jake, knowing you didn't love me," Julia whispered.

Jake gathered her into his arms. What could this sweet woman possibly have done that would keep him from loving her?

"I'll always love you, Julia." He kissed the hair near her temple. "We'll be mad and argue, I'm sure, but love's forever. When you're ready to talk, you let me know."

Jake could not get Julia's comments out of his head. They had both declared their love. It had been heartfelt and sincere. What would make her think he wouldn't love her forever? He said he would. And as she should know by now, his word was gospel. Julia had a haunted look about her as he left her bed. About a terror she'd held inside for a long time. He knew she was no virgin when she came to his bed. She'd told him. What else would a woman like Julia have in her past that would make her tremble so? Jake shrugged off his misgivings and concentrated on patching the barn roof he'd started this morning. He whistled a tune. It was a beautiful fall day, and he was in love with his wife.

* * *

Julia's days blended together. She helped Flossie make jelly and made baby clothes for her new nephew. And she fell deeper in love with her husband than she'd ever thought possible. Her letters to her family were never answered. With the crops in, Jake concentrated on getting the farm ready for winter. He came home every night for dinner, dirty, sweating and smiling. They made love more nights than not, and Julia reveled in his body and to her surprise, her own. Memories of feeling displaced and unloved faded. Julia didn't allow herself to think often of Boston. It was too painful. And she knew full well, she'd been blessed when she began to correspond with Jacob Snelling. Oh, how she wished she were carrying Jake's child. She knew he wanted a family.

"Do you think there's something the matter with me, Flossie?" Julia asked her sister-in-law one day late in November. Flossie had brought the children over, and Julia was teaching them to speak French. The lesson was done for the day, and Millie and Danny had run outside.

Flossie straightened from looking in the oven. "Are you sick, Julia?"

Julia shook her head. "No. I was just wondering why I've not gotten pregnant."

"No, I don't think there's anything the matter with you. But if you're worried go see the doc. You've only been married six months. Some folks take longer than others."

Julia shrugged and looked out the window, head in her hand. "I know. It's just that I know Jake wants a family so much. I want to give one to him."

Flossie sat down beside Julia. "Julia, my brother is happier than he's been in years. I know he wants a baby, and you do, too. But seeing him the way he is now, well, I think it's just fine for the two of you to be happy all on your own for awhile."

"I am happy, Flossie," Julia said with a smile. "I didn't think I could ever be this happy." If only she knew how Jillian was doing at boarding school. If only she could talk to the girl or hear from her. "If only . . ."

"If only what, Julia?" Flossie asked.

"Nothing. Now tell me what kind of dress we're going to make Millie for Christmas."

* * *

Julia decided to wait one more month and then go see Dr. Hammish. Most likely Flossie was right. Some folks just take longer than others. Right now, she and her sister-in-laws had lots to do to get ready for the Christmas holiday. There were gifts for the children, and gifts for each other and recipes and decorations to think of. This would be a bitter sweet holiday for her. She looked forward to spending the holiday with Jake and his family. But this would be the first year she had not celebrated with Jillian.

And the more Julia thought and planned about her first Christmas in South Dakota the more she missed Jillian. She worried about her at her new school. She wondered if her Mother gave Jillian her letters or the girl thought Julia had completely abandoned her. This ache was gnawing at her and would not let go.

The wind was blowing snow horizontal to the barren fields Julia could see out of her kitchen window. The kitchen was toasty warm and smelled like cinnamon. There was a stack of cookies in the middle of the table, and Julia had draped fresh pine over the door frame. Julia was as happy and miserable as she'd ever thought she'd be.

She had gone to town with Flossie the day before to see Dr. Hammish. Flossie had picked up a letter addressed to Julia while she was in Snelling's General Store. Julia fingered the letter while she waited for Dr. Hammish to see her. The return address was her Boston home, but she did not recognize the handwriting. She slid her nail under the seal and looked at the last page first. It was from Eustace and apparently written by the woman's daughter. Eustace's mother was failing fast. Life with the Crawfords was much the same and Jennifer was being hotly courted by a young man Eustace had seen at the last party. Jillian, however, was very unhappy at school. The last time she had been allowed to come home from Ramsey for a weekend, she had either kept to her room or gotten into an argument with a family member or a servant.

Julia buried the letter in her bag and gone in to see the waiting doctor. When the kindly old man had announced that she'd be presenting Jake with a child next summer, she had burst into tears.

"What's the matter, dear?" Dr. Hammish asked. "These don't look like happy tears to me."

Julia wiped her eyes and took a deep breath. "I'm happier than you can imagine. Just awfully emotional. That happens, doesn't it?"

"Yes, it does," he said. "You'll feel a whole lot better when you get home and tell Jake. You want me to call Flossie in?"

"No," Julia said. "I want to tell Jake first."

"Then it will be our secret," he said. "Eat right. Don't go lifting something too heavy, and make sure you get back in town to see me in a month."

Julia made the ride home in silence, only answering Flossie's questions with a shake of her head. Every bit of joy she felt was at odds with how low she was feeling about Jillian.

* * *

Jake came into the kitchen, stomped his feet and shook his head like a dog. The house was warm and smelled

145

good. He grabbed two cookies from the plate on the table on the way to kiss his wife.

"Hey, darling," he said as picked Julia up and twirled her around. "I'm glad to be out of that weather and in here with you. The house looks real nice. What's the matter?" he asked. "Why you crying?"

Julia laid her head against his chest. "I was thinking about my sisters back in Boston. We always loved Christmas."

"Then why don't we plan on going to see them once the crops are in this spring. We'll make it a belated honeymoon," he said.

"You'd go see my family after how rude they were to you?" she asked.

Jake bent his head down to see Julia's face. He'd dread going to visit the Crawfords. He didn't think he'd ever known anyone as conniving and duplicitous than her mother and father. Paying his hands to leave and sashaying into his house making Julia feel like a child and expecting her to board the train back to Boston. There was some secret deceit, too. Just what, he'd not figured out. But he'd endure a visit for her if that's what she wanted. Lately Julia hadn't been her usual cheerful self. Not smiling and gay like he'd become accustomed to. She had been crying at night when she thought he was asleep. Nearly tore his heart in two to hear her suffer.

"Sure, honey. If it makes you happy," Jake said. Julia wobbled a smile.

* * *

Julia rested her head against Jake's chest. He was all solid warmth. His arms held her, and he rubbed lazy circles on her back. She had waited six months to tell Jake she was pregnant and now that the time had arrived, she could not bring herself to tell him. How would she explain how unhappy she was?

The door flew open and Flossie and the kids burst through the door.

"It's freezing out there, Uncle Jake," Danny said.

"What are you doing out riding around in this weather," Jake said. "Harry will kill you."

"Me and the kids are fine. Snow's stopping anyway," Flossie said.

Julia helped Danny and Millie off with their coats and Flossie was pouring a cup of coffee.

"What brought you over, Flossie?" Julia asked as she handed each child a cookie.

Flossie pulled a letter from inside her coat. "When I got home yesterday I sat down to read the letter from Harry's sister. There were two letters there. I didn't realize." Flossie was grinning ear to ear. "The other one's another letter for you. I know the one you got from your friend the cleaning woman made you sad. I just know this one's going to be good news."

"You got a letter from home, Julia?" Jake asked.

"Eustace's mother is dying. And Jillian is very unhappy at school," Julia said and looked up at her husband. She'd been so preoccupied with the news of Jillian and finding out she was expecting, she'd forgotten to tell Jake about Eustace's letter.

"You've been waiting for months for word from them. I just kind of thought you'd have told me," Jake said.

"Bad news is no fun to share. But this letter is good news," Flossie said. "I can feel it in my bones."

"Is it a letter from the sister at school, Aunt Julia?" Millie asked.

Julia shook her head and turned the letter over in her hand. The writing was clearly Jane Crawford's. Jake slipped his arm around her shoulder and kissed the top of her head.

"Maybe you want to read your letter alone. Up in our bedroom. Then you can tell us all the news," Jake said.

Julia climbed the steps without a word or glance to anyone standing in the kitchen. She closed her bedroom door, opened the curtains and wrapped a shawl around her shoulders. She pulled the old rocker near the window and sat down. Julia turned the envelope over and over in her hand. Desperate for news. Unwilling to submit herself to her mother's censure. She would have no happy news to share with Flossie and Jake she was sure. Julia lifted the edge of envelope with her nail and saw her mother's cream-colored stationary inside. Julia opened the letter with shaking hands.

Dear Julia,

Your behavior and appearance during our visit was shocking to your father and me to say the least. How you could have deemed life on a farm preferable to your home and family in Boston is hard to imagine. And a farmer of all things, Julia. Although he seems attentive enough. Remember, though, it will not last. Whatever you have done or are doing to gain this man's attentions will fade soon enough. I am telling you this with your best interest at heart.

Jennifer sends her greeting. Jolene as well. Although your older sister bears the brunt of the embarrassing questions regarding your absence.

I received a letter from Jillian of late. She sends her regards as well. And wished me to pass on to you some message concerning a Mrs. Beechly. The woman is alive and well. Hopefully this is not more of Jillian's make-believe nonsense. Her time at school would be best spent studying and making friends with girls of similar families. Remember Jolene met Turner's sister at that school not so many years ago.

Perhaps Jillian needs to understand the great gift your father and I give her by sending her to Ramsey. A girl in her position will need every connection necessary for a rewarding future. A dose of reality may be what Jillian needs to hear to understand her position in this family and her good fortune. Undowered girls, even beautiful ones struggle on occasion.

I must close this letter for there is much left for me to do regarding the party your father and I are hosting this weekend. Eustace's mother died and many of the details have fallen to me.

Mother

The letter shook wildly in Julia's hands. Tears smudged the loops of her mother's writing. Eustace's mother had died. And Jillian's only message to Julia was about Mrs. Beechly. How miserable and desperate was the girl? Did Julia's mother intended to mold Jillian to her specifications by shaking the very foundation of the girl's existence. Was the implied threat her intention? Or the final gesture to make Julia come home? Could Julia risk it by calling her mother's bluff? And possibly leave Jillian alone to face and understand all that was said? Could she leave Flossie and Millie and return to Boston? Leave Will and Harry and Gloria. Never see Danny or little Joshua again? Could she leave Jake?

Julia dropped to her knees in front of the smoldering fireplace. She poked the ashes to life viciously. Her shoulders shook with hysteria and she feared she would vomit. Julia rolled each page of her mother's stationary into balls and threw them each into the ashes. She curled up on her side, her back to the fire as fresh tears surfaced.

* * *

Jake, Flossie and Millie ate dinner in silence. Julia had not come down stairs. Flossie kissed her brother goodbye and left. Jake sat at the kitchen table, drumming his fingers, wondering what to do. The silence was more unnerving, more overwhelming than any shouting could have been. Jake didn't want to intrude on Julia. He knew from experience that sometimes the only hope of a solution was found in silence. Whether prayer or contemplation, he didn't really know what to call what he did, but he knew when life's trials threatened, a good long look at a sunset or even a blank wall seemed to point his mind in the direction he needed to take. Maybe Julia was deciding to ask him for help or advice. He'd surely give it. Whatever that family of hers were feuding about caused his sweet wife a lot of pain.

Jake glanced at his pocket watch. Six o'clock. Flossie and the kids were long gone and Julia had been upstairs nearly three hours. He knocked softly at their bedroom door and got no response. Jake turned the knob and peaked in the room. She was not in their bed. Julia was not in the rocker he had heard squeaks from earlier in the day. Jake stopped with a start, stunned at what he saw.

His wife was curled tight as a ball on the cold stone hearth. What could her mother have said in the letter for his wife to lie down there, with their bed feet away? Jake knelt and swept the hair from her face. Julia's shoulders shrugged in her sleep, and she grimaced. Dried tear tracks marred Julia's face that was tense and painful even in slumber. Jake picked her up, kissed her forehead and lay her down on the bed. He stared at her, his gut clenching. His own problems in the past had been difficult. But none of them caused the pain he was feeling now. Watching Julia suffer harkened back to how he felt when Flossie got cut. He picked up the now empty envelope from Jane Crawford. Poison mailed the whole way from Boston. Touching the hands and mind of the woman he loved. Jake turned to the fireplace. He picked up Julia's shawl from where it lay in a heap. And then he saw them.

Tightly curled wads of paper amongst the ashes. Cold ashes. Julia had meant to burn the letter he was sure. He stared at the stationary and then knelt to retrieve it. Jake turned the balls of paper over and over in his hand. Curiosity killed the cat was what folks said. But were those folks watching someone they cared about, loved being torn apart inside? Jake flattened the paper out on the dresser and read.

Chapter Twelve

ULIA AWOKE AS THE SKY turned from a brilliant blue to an orange glow. She stared out the window, her eyes gritty from tears. Hysteria had not solved her problem. The solace of sleep held escape only as long as her eyes were closed and her mind unconscious. Julia looked over the blankets when she realized she was not alone in her room. Jake stood, leaning against the wall, watching her. Studying her.

"I'm sorry I didn't come back downstairs. Mother's letter was . . . disturbing."

"Why would your parents leave your youngest sister without a dowry?" he asked.

Julia's eyes widened. She looked at the crumpled papers in his hand. "You had no right."

Jake nodded. "You're right. You're absolutely right. But then it's not everyday a man finds his wife curled in a ball on a stone hearth. The only news she receives from home in months, meant for ashes."

Julia sat up. "There was nothing extraordinary in the letter. Nothing I couldn't relay to you or Flossie from memory."

Jake stalked the bed. "You flattened the dandelion Millie gave you in a book, Julia. And a letter from home is crushed and thrown in the fire?" Jake shook his head. "Give me a little more credit than that. What kind of position is your sister in that she needs to make 'connections'? And who is Mrs. Beechley?"

Julia's lip trembled. She should have told Jake the story when she didn't love him. It would have been easier. Yet she couldn't remember a time here she didn't love him.

"Mrs. Beechley was my make-believe friend when I was a child." Julia dropped her eyes. "One night when Jillian couldn't fall asleep I told her. Jillian sort of adopted her. I often saw her talking to thin air. As she got older, Jillian and I got closer, and she didn't mention Mrs. Beechley very often."

Jake shook his head. "Why would that make you so upset? So Jillian has a vivid imagination? That's what made you cry yourself to sleep?"

Julia shook her head. "No. As Jillian got older she only mentioned Mrs. Beechley when she was horribly upset. She must be devastated to risk passing that message through my mother." Julia looked up at Jake, misery in her eyes, on her face and in her heart. "Jillian's telling me she's very unhappy. Wretched, in fact."

"And you're far away. Too far to do anything for her."

Julia nodded and looked out the window. "She's alone at a school. Away from home. Probably suffering like I did when I was there. It was horrible."

"Why did your parents make her go there if you had such a horrible time of it?"

"Ramsey Academy for Young Ladies is the school where all the best families send their daughters. Everyone there is from a wealthy, influential family. Where the connections are made for the best marriages between those families. Where young girls are educated in all the necessary social skills to control those around them. Where they learn to be cruel."

"Why would you parents leave their youngest child undowered?"

Reckoning time had arrived, as Eustace would have said. Jake had married a woman he didn't know and wouldn't have wanted to if he'd been privy to the Crawford skeletons.

"Jillian is not my parents' daughter."

"But they've raised her as one." Jake said. "She obviously doesn't know she's not their daughter." He stared at her. "Your mother is threatening to tell her."

All Julia could do was nod and swallow.

Jake turned, stared out the window and turned back to Julia quickly. "Who's daughter is she, Julia?"

"Mine," Julia whispered.

"Turner Crenshaw," he said.

"My mother and I took a year long trip shortly after Jolene's wedding. Jillian was born in South Carolina."

Jake shook his head. "So you stood at the altar, carrying the groom's child. But you were not the bride."

Julia swallowed. "Yes."

"And after all these years your parents decide to withhold an inheritance from a girl they've raised since infancy. This is unbelievable."

"It was not my parent's idea. My father, in fact, held out for quite a while." Julia met Jake's amazed look grimly. "Jolene did not think our family holdings should be split four ways rather than three. If Jillian was entitled, then her children should be as well."

"I thought Turner had money? Your parents are as rich as Croesus. How much God damned money does your sister need?"

Julia cringed. Jake was screaming. "There were only three daughters . . ."

"Don't defend them. Don't ever defend them," Jake shouted. "If the decision was made to raise Jillian as their own then, damn it, she's their daughter. No matter how much your older sister whines." Jake dropped into the chair near the window to whisper. "Who are you, Julia?"

"I know. I had a child out of wedlock. Turner was the first man to pay attention to me. It was so stupid. So childish. I am so sorry. I wish I had waited for our wedding night. I wanted that so much. Especially now." Julia stopped talking and her crying dwindled to hiccoughs as she watched Jake's face. It had turned from astonishment to disbelief and finally to anger. He had married a woman so beneath him. A woman who allowed her chastity to be stolen for a few moments of attention.

"I am so sorry," she said.

Jake stood slowly and walked to the door of their room. "I could care less you had a child out of wedlock. You were what, seventeen? Mistakes happen. You left your own child, your own flesh and blood at the mercy of the vipers you call a family. Like as if I'd have ever left Gloria outside on the porch waiting for a wolf to tear her in two." He met her eyes then. "Thank God you're not pregnant. I don't want any child of mine to suffer like Jillian if you get it in your head to leave us someday."

Julia sat in stunned silence. Jake had long ago left their bedroom. The impact of Jake's words had left her mind blank and her body still. Julia knew, knew instinctively, that if she allowed herself to consider Jake's words she would be forced to face the worst of her secrets. She had been successful all these years locking away without consideration what Jake had just said.

In dark moments, when sleep would not come and self-doubt, hysteria and paranoia crept around her thoughts like a fog, she had refused to succumb. Refused to voice or even think about how incredibly weak she had been. If she allowed that self-loathing to surface then Julia was sure she would drown in a vast lake of regrets. The thought of facing those regrets, more terrifying than throwing herself under the wheels of a train. That pain would be fleeting. Death would erase that worldly burden. Life, her life, viewed as an observer, would deliver heartache for an insurmountable number of years.

But the review would not dim, not now, not after Jake's words. And Julia's greatest failing had been weakness. Julia had squandered the God given instinct to protect that which was born of her womb. Even dogs guarded their young. But not Julia Crawford, she thought to herself grimly as she stared at a knot on the wall. She had done exactly as Jake had said. Julia had left her own daughter to the manipulations and pain of her mother and Jolene. But what could she have done? Dare she bring Jillian with her to South Dakota? Julia shook her head. It wasn't this home that Julia had denied her daughter. It was any home. She should have stood up to her mother years ago, even if it meant living in a tenement. Or with her aunt. Or anywhere.

Julia was wholly unworthy of the paper slipped between her the leather casings of her suitcase. Jillian's birth certificate. She had no right to lay claim to the girl or the creased parchment. Or the words. *Mother: Julia Crawford, Father: Unknown.* What if at this moment Jane Crawford stood before her frightened daughter to bear witness to Julia's shame? Then her greatest fear would be realized. Jillian would know then her own mother was too cowardly to protect her. Had instead boarded a train to leave her heartache behind. Had instead chosen escape. Julia knew then the pathetic reality she had feared was out of the tightly closed box of her conscience.

"Thank God you're not pregnant" Jake had said. And those words were surely the reason Julia had no recollection of that night nor how she found herself at the kitchen table the following morning. Jake had never come to bed. No other night had she needed his arms more, but he had not come. There was no coffee made and his coat was not on the hook by the door. Had he left early that morning? Or last night and never come home? It didn't really matter. He was as gone from this house as he was from her heart.

A shadow fell over the table and Julia looked up. "Flossie, I didn't hear you come in."

Jake's sister bustled around the kitchen, silently. She made coffee and poured two cups. Flossie sat one in front of Julia and took hers to the sink. "Jake stayed with Harry and me last night."

Julia held her coffee mug but did not drink or speak.

"He told me everything, Julia. He probably shouldn't have, but he did."

Flossie knew. This woman she respected and come to love and admire knew what a useless woman Julia really was. Flossie would have died before allowing anything to happen to Millie or Danny. Julia was not worthy to sit at the table with her let alone call her family. Julia could not look her in the eye.

"I don't know what to say."

Flossie pulled out a chair and sat down. "You think your mother will actually tell Jillian this whole story while she's away at school and you're here."

"I'm not sure. But the threat is there for certain." Tears filled Julia's eyes. "I wish I could stop her. Do something. But I . . ."

"What are you going to do?" Flossie asked.

Julia shrugged. "There's little I can do."

Flossie grabbed Julia's hand. "What are you going to do, Julia?"

Julia stared at Flossie through the dim blur of tears. "I can't. I'm not strong like you. I . . . I"

"You'll be every bit as strong as you need to be," Flossie said.

"I can't do it," Julia cried.

"You've made this old shack a home, Julia. You've harvested corn and delivered my sister's baby. You've driven a wagon and taught my kids French and read them books. You've washed clothes and made them." Flossie stopped to swipe her hand over her eyes. "You've shown my brother that happiness was meant for him too, damn it." Flossie's voice rose and quivered. "Don't call yourself a weakling, Julia Shelling. I won't let you."

Julia's lip trembled. "But I can't make bread. Or butter. I can't . . ."

Flossie grabbed Julia's shoulders and shook. "Do you think Millie or Danny would care if I couldn't cook? Do you think they'd love Harry any less if he couldn't build a fence? Children don't care. They know we're there for them. That's what they care about."

Julia stood and screamed back all the frustration and hurt trapped inside. "Don't you see? That's just it. I haven't been there. Ever. How much would Millie or Danny love you if you left them?"

"And if I had one ounce, one instant of life left in me, I'd do what I could to right a wrong to my children. I'd die trying. I don't believe you don't feel the same way about Jillian."

Long minutes passed before Julia's stomach settled and she sat down. "My mother would never allow a scandal of this magnitude to touch our family. They'd never let me take her."

"They adopted her then?"

Julia shook her head. "No. It was never necessary."

"Where's the birth certificate?"

"Upstairs in my valise."

Flossie touched Julia's face and smiled. "Then there's little they can do, Julia. Don't you see? You don't have to worry anymore what they think of you or what they say to you. She's your daughter. Claim her."

Julia's lip trembled. "What will Jillian think of me? After all these years."

"The years come and go, Julia. Do you want anymore of them to go by without Jillian knowing who her mother is?"

Julia shook her head. "I don't want another minute to escape me. I've missed so much already." Julia twisted her hanky in her hand. The thought of the unthinkable was borrowing into her gut. Could she do it? Face her family? Face Jillian?

"Where would I go? Jake won't want me back." There it was. Said aloud. Her pitiful accommodations to her family's reputation had cost her the one thing other than Jillian that she cherished.

"My brother's stubborn as they come. And your announcement knocked his feet out from under him. I told him it wasn't fitting for him to judge you. He didn't know what you went through everyday. He screamed and hollered and sent Harry and the kids scurrying out to see the chickens." Flossie said. "I'm not afraid of my brother. Never have been. I told him to sit down and shut up."

"I can't imagine he took kindly to that reasoning." Julia said. "He does have the right to judge me. I'm his wife, and I've deceived him from the moment I said 'I do'."

Flossie arched her brow. "I told him he took a hell of a risk all those years ago. Three kids running a farm. He thought he was doing the right thing, and so did you. You thought Jillian would have a better life as your parents' daughter than as yours."

"Oh, Flossie. He still feels guilty about your accident. Don't make him feel worse."

"I didn't try to. But, Julia, things happen. Accidents happen along the way of life. And sometimes the path we take isn't of our own choosing. We start out in one direction, whether by aim or need, and the trail gets deeper and narrower and more familiar." Flossie stared at Julia and continued. "And we just stay the course. You did what you thought was best. I think you know better now. This is your chance to change your route."

"You're more a sister me than any sister I have, Flossie. I don't know what I'm going to do yet," Julia said as she wobbled a smile, "but I'm going to do something."

Flossie hugged Julia. "I'm a new aunt, and I don't even know what the child looks like."

Julia dragged Flossie to the spare bedroom where her unpacked trunk was. She was going to show off her daughter for the first time ever in her life. It was a most miraculous feeling.

"Here she is," Julia said and wiped her eyes. "Isn't she beautiful?"

Flossie held the miniature in her hand and touched the face painted there. "She's the picture of her mother. Very lovely."

Julia took the small, framed picture in her hand and smiled as she stared. She looked up to Flossie with resolve. "This is my daughter."

Julia sat on the bed clutching the picture of Jillian long after she heard the door slam as Flossie left. She wavered from over whelming guilt to despair. One glance at Jillian's face forced conviction from somewhere deep down inside to rise up, shouting to be heard. *I can do this. I will do this. I have to do this.* Julia needed to win this battle, the prize being her own flesh and blood. If she had learned nothing else from Jake, it was this sentiment.

Family first. Above all else. And Jillian was her daughter. The nine months Julia carried her gave her the right. Jake and his family had given her the will.

* * *

Julia begged Slim to take her to town that afternoon. She stayed at the hotel till the next morning and boarded the first eastbound train that had come through. Julia may no longer be worthy of her husband and his family, may sicken her husband in fact, but she stubbornly clung to the life time of love she and Jillian shared. Flossie was right. If it took till her dying breath to convince Jillian of her love, then so be it. What it would cost was the love and respect of her husband.

Julia stared out the window of the train as it chugged and churned through the Pennsylvania landscape. She loved Jake. She'd been fortunate indeed to have his love for the brief time that she'd had. No tears came to Julia's eyes for love lost. Her tears had been shed as she smelled his pillow and hugged it. Julia left their bedroom, refusing to look at the fruit of her work for Jake's home before climbing into the wagon. This was not the time for childish reactions. She was an adult. Julia knew she needed her wits and sensibilities about her to retrieve her daughter.

Had she stayed with Jake, had she let herself cry or bemoan her vast problems, had she let herself be content with her life's path, Julia was certain she'd die a bitter and miserable woman. Jake and his family had changed her. She had hope however slim. She had a thread of confidence in herself. And she had an overwhelming urge to hug her daughter. Kiss her hair and tell her that her mother would make things all right.

Jake would think the worst of her that was certain. She'd left no explanation for him. Julia had written a letter to Flossie and given it to Slim to deliver. With little doubt her heart would miss Jake every day of her life. But she also knew he was right and that she had been terribly wrong. He would have never left a child. And worse than the knowledge that Jake could no longer love her was the idea of seeing his face everyday, filled with disappointment and wariness rather than the smile she'd grown to cherish.

* * *

Jake rode his fences and property lines all day. He was still in shock. Julia was a mother. She had left her own child in the clutches of her mother. Jake hadn't realized the depth of his hatred for the Crawfords till then. They had bullied Julia, threatened her, run off his ranch hands and now had Jillian in their sights. What would a ten-year-old think finding out her mother wasn't whom she thought all along?

His feelings about his wife were more complicated. There was no clear-cut line. Not all disgust. Not mostly love. A mass mix of empathy and disappointment for

Julia. She had been forced to stand at the altar of her sister's wedding, expecting a child with the groom. But Julia had lived with their manipulations all of her life. How could she in good conscience, knowing what she did, leave her own child mired in that family? He would have still married her, child or not. Jake scowled at himself and pulled his horse to halt. He wouldn't have married her. If Julia had been standing at the train station with Jillian, Jake would have known she wasn't Inga.

God had led him on this path, to this woman for a reason. Who was he to deny it? It would take some sorting out, some leeway and time on his part, but he figured he'd might as well accept facts as they were. Who was he to cast stones as Flossie had asked?

He did not understand his wife at all and wasn't sure he trusted her. Julia had left her own child elsewhere. To marry a shopkeeper. What assurances would he have that Julia wouldn't leave him and any child they may have? None. Jake reluctantly admitted that might be the crux of the problem. He had fallen desperately in love with his wife. Julia loved her daughter, of that he was certain. It explained her daydreams and tears and joy when Jillian's name was mentioned. Julia loved the girl and still left. Bringing Jake's thoughts full circle. Was Julia's love strong enough to make her stay?

Jake had his answer hours later. He had ridden and thought and worked enough to sort out his feelings. He would try and forget what Julia had done. Try not to judge. It wasn't going to be easy. Jake knew that. He wondered if there'd ever be a time he'd ride in from the fields not worried whether his wife would be there. Or whether she'd gone. But nothing compared to the sick feeling in his heart as he walked in the darkened kitchen that evening. Nothing in his life prepared him for the dread he felt as he inched up the steps calling Julia's name. His voice echoed in the stairway. There was no answer. Jake's deepest fears had been realized.

Chapter Thirteen

ULIA NEEDED A PLAN, AND it had formed by the time she pulled into the Boston train station. Her first stop was The National Bank. Julia waited patiently, although travel-weary for Mr. Flemming to emerge from his office.

"Julia, dear, what a pleasant surprise. Your father told me you were on an extended holiday with relatives."

Julia smiled at the rotund man, a lifelong friend of her father's and frequent visitor at the Market Street house as she attempted to battle her shaking nerves. "I was away Mr. Flemming. It is good to see you as well." Julia took a deep breath. "May we speak in your office?"

"Why of course, my dear. Is everything all right? I don't have a meeting with your father I've forgotten, do

I?" Harold Flemming took Julia's elbow and escorted her into his richly-appointed office.

"No, I don't believe so," Julia said. She met the man's eyes to gauge his reaction. "I've come on business of my own." Harold Flemming's face was a mask of pleasantries but not before Julia caught his surprised look. Julia stared at the brass buttons of the green leather chair as he sank into it.

"What can I help you with today, Julia?"

Julia wound the taupe string of her bag around her finger. "I would like to know the amount of money I have at my disposal." Julia dropped her head, took a deep breath and stared evenly at Mr. Flemming's curious eyes. "The amount that I have access to without a signature from my parents."

Flemming's bushy white brows shot up. He said nothing.

"I know my grandparents left me a small amount and that my father always deposited what he called our pin money in that account. Can you tell me how much that is?"

Harold Flemming stood and came around the desk, perching his girth near Julia. "If you are in some trouble, my dear, maybe your father should be here."

These were the moments Julia dreaded all of her life. The subtle control couched in a concern for her best interests. She rubbed the picture of Jillian through her satin bag. This was not a moment for weakness. Jake had not been weak when that dreadful Mr. Smith had threatened. Jake protected and kept what was his.

"I believe," Julia began and stopped to clear her throat. "I believe that an account with my name only makes me a client of this bank. Is that not correct, Mr. Flemming?" She continued at his nod but before his sputtering could take hold. "As a client of National Bank, I believe, I'm entitled to know the amount in my account. And with the discretion you would afford any client."

Mr. Flemming's open mouth closed slowly. He stood and went to the door of his office. Julia heard him confer with his secretary. He returned to his seat behind a massive cherry desk, file in hand.

"You are absolutely right, Julia. As a client, you are entitled to all the things you mentioned." Flemming tilted his head. "But as a family friend who has watched you grow from a young child, I feel obligated to be sure you are not in some sort of trouble. Something you feel you need to hide from your family." Julia said nothing. Flemming slowly opened the yellow folder, tilted his glasses and read. "Ten thousand, four hundred and eighty three dollars, including this month's interest."

It was no fortune. But it was no piddling amount either. "I would like to withdraw ten thousand dollars," Julia said.

Flemming looked at Julia with barely concealed anger. "Really Julia. I hardly in good conscience can allow you to withdraw this amount of money in cash. Let alone let you walk into your father's home carrying it. William Crawford would be furious and rightfully so."

"I won't be staying with my parents."

Flemming removed his glasses and rubbed a beefy hand down his face. "That is hardly the point, Julia. You are an unmarried woman. Unescorted."

"There must be a way other customers have access to their money without meeting the bank president each time, Mr. Flemming. What would you do for such a client?"

"I suppose we could transfer the funds to a signature account," Flemming replied. "That is how most of our customers do it. Then you can go to a teller, show him your account book and withdraw funds." Harold Flemming tilted his head and smiled benignly. "I just hope, as does your father, that you're not intending to well, perhaps grant someone a loan or a gift. Someone who's made certain promises." Flemming leaned over the desk to whisper. "Someone unworthy of your attentions."

It was becoming clear to Julia. Flemming assumed the fat old maid of the Crawford clan was bewitched by a shyster. A handsome shyster who preyed on unmarried rich woman. A shyster she would have to buy to hold his attention. Julia understood Flemming's concerns much more than he would have thought she would. These situations were explained fully at Ramsey. Poor men sometimes attached themselves to rich woman, promising romance and adventure to get their hands on a fortune.

Julia could hear Miss Priscilla Montique, her decorum instructor, speaking as if she were in the room. *"We must guard ourselves and the work of our family against those not in the same social strata as the esteemed families you have all come from. Remember, gentlemen never mention money in the presence of a lady."* Julia had no intention of explaining her need for money to Harold Flemming. He would trip over his coattails to get to William Crawford's ear.

"I appreciate your concern. It is nothing like what you imagine. However, I believe I am entitled to spend my money in any fashion I see fit." Julia was shaking. She had stood her ground. But what chance did she have of getting to one red cent without the banker's approval.

Flemming sat back in his chair and stared intensely. He put his glasses back on taking time to fit the wire spectacles behind his ears. Without looking up he replied, "Very well. I will have Mr. Cummings make the arrangements."

Julia let out a breath she didn't realize she'd been holding. "Thank you very much."

Flemming showed Julia to Mr. Cummings desk and made his goodbyes. Julia was glad to see him walk down the carpeted hallway. Maybe then she could focus on what Mr. Cummings was telling her and less on the sound of her own heartbeat.

Julia left the bank with one hundred dollars in cash and a small black leather book detailing her withdrawal. As she stood on the busy Boston street, Julia stood straighter as she looked at the teaming mass making their way past her. Men tipped their hats as Julia made her way to the edge of the sidewalk. A smile crossed her lips, as she held tighter to her reticule, her one hundred dollars tucked inside. Now if she could just hail one of the leather cabs lined up to take businessmen to their destinations. She looked left and right around the shoulders of men shouting and waving to drivers. A man glanced down at her, pulled his hat from his head and smiled.

"Are you in need of assistance, miss?"

Julia flashed the man a gleaming smile on the heels of her success with Mr. Flemming. "Why, yes, sir. I am need of a driver. Could you help me?"

The man fumbled with his hat and elbowed other men aside. "Make way, you there, make way. This lady needs a cabbie." He turned to Julia and held the side of the carriage. He held out his hand. "Allow me."

"Would you be so kind as to give the driver this address?" Julia asked.

Julia pulled up to her destination, paid the driver and knocked on the door of the small house in a crowded section of town. Black faces, young and old watched her as she stood on the step of the brick tenement. A small girl cracked the door and peered out at Julia.

"Hello. You must be Mary. Is your mother home?"

* * *

Jake sat on his porch steps until the sun sank far below the horizon. If he'd been thinking of anything but Julia, he'd have known his hands were near frozen. The men stared at him from the bunkhouse window. Finally, Jake noticed Slim making his way towards him.

"Evening, boss."

"Slim."

Slim pulled his coat tightly around him and his hat from his head. Looking around as if waiting for something to happen. "Tain't none of my business, I reckon', but we's been a wondering what you're doing sittin' out here in the cold."

Jake stared past him.

"Have anything to do with the Missus taking a trip?"

Jake eyed him. "What do you know about that?"

Slim's lip curled up under his nose. He shook his head. "Yep, I was a wonderin'."

Jake kept his voice even. "What do you know about my wife, Slim?"

"Well, I was the one that took her to town. Such a sweet, pretty little thing, Mrs. Shelling. Always so nice to me and the boys. Made doilies for under our kerosene . . ."

Before Jake realized what he'd done he was holding Slim a foot off the ground by his coat. "You took her to town."

Jake dropped Slim to his feet and rubbed his head. "Sorry, Slim. Don't suppose you'd be wanting to tell me where she went?" Damn it. He shouldn't care where she went. It shouldn't matter. Jake turned to the porch to go inside. He was cold as hell now. From the inside out. "Never mind, Slim. Sorry." He was nearly inside when Slim's words stopped him.

"Said she had a little girl back in Boston. Showed me her picture and everything. Near tears, touching that beautiful little girl's face on that there portrait. Said she'd spent too much time away from the child." Slim stared and waited for his boss's reply. "She bringin' the little one here, then?"

"It sounds like you know more of my wife's plans than I do. I don't have the foggiest notion what she'll do." Jake let the door slam behind him. So after ten years Julia was finally going to do the right thing. He wished she'd have told him her plans. A knock at the door sounded. Jake pulled it open. Slim stood on the stoop holding a letter.

"Mrs. Shelling asked me to deliver this to Mrs. Marks. I hain't had no time to ride out to your sister's place. Mebbe you'll be seeing her first," Slim said as he held the letter out to Jake.

Jake took the letter, nodded to Slim and closed the door. One thing he knew for sure, he wasn't about to open it. He'd learned his lesson about reading what hadn't been intended for his eyes. But he wasn't the one to leave a child alone with a pack of wolves. Julia started this mess long before he met her. The day she handed her own flesh and blood over to her mother. On that thought he could get good and mad. Jake grabbed the whiskey from under the sink and took a swig. By the time the bottle was near empty, Jake had himself mad as hell at Julia. Cursing her for everything short of the War Between the States. And being mad was a whole hell of a lot easier than being sad, Jake thought as he stared at the doily under the bowl of wild flowers on his kitchen table.

* * *

Flossie found Jake the next morning asleep on his hands at the kitchen table, clutching a letter. She shook his shoulder softly and then spied the empty whiskey bottle.

"Jake, wake up. It's eight o'clock," she shouted.

Jake lifted one eye open to see his sister's angry face. "Let me alone."

Flossie harrumphed and proceeded to make as much noise as possible while she brewed coffee. She slammed the old enamel pot down on the stove. She pushed in kitchen chairs with a slam. Each time Jake's head lifted off the table with a groan. Finally, Flossie opened a window to let the cold November air spill into the kitchen. When her brother didn't stir, she pulled on her coat.

"Close the God-dammed window, Flossie."

Flossie stopped, hand on the doorknob. "Close it yourself. Or freeze to death. Makes no never mind to me."

"This letter's for you."

Flossie walked to the table and waited for Jake to lift his head. "From Julia? Did you read this one, too?"

"Shut up, Flossie and get me some coffee," Jake growled.

Flossie took off her coat and sat down. She watched her brother, now sitting up white-faced, stare at the envelope. He handed it to her slowly as if the letting go was more significant than the mere passing of paper. Flossie took the letter, tucked it in her apron and rose to pour Jake a cup of coffee.

"Drink the whole pot. Clean yourself and this house up too. We're celebrating Millie's birthday on Sunday. Eating at one," Flossie said as she shrugged her coat back on.

"Aren't you going to read it?" Jake asked. He dropped his pleading eyes from Flossie's face. "Forget it. Doesn't matter what it says." Jake stood slowly and clutched the back of the chair until the room stopped spinning.

"I'll read it when I get home, Jake. It is addressed to me."

"Fine, fine, do whatever you want," Jake said as he made his way to the staircase.

Flossie watched Jake climb the steps. He was as stubborn and proud, as he was loyal and honest. Thick-headed and smart all rolled into one man. And happy as hell for the short while that Julia was here. Flossie gathered the children from Slim's watch and headed her wagon home to read.

Jake spent the rest of the week quietly. He didn't leave the house much. Told Slim he was feeling poorly. And that he was. He'd never told a soul how much Valerie Morton's betrayal had hurt him although he imagined Flossie suspected. That pain had a lot to do with hurt pride and disappointment for well-laid plans gone awry. This pain was ten times bigger and reached past his pride. All the way to his heart. He should have never told Julia he loved her. Never should have admitted it to himself. Should have stuck to his plan of a good cook and sons. Should've never let himself be caught up as Julia turned his house into a home. Never let himself plan to see her smile at the end of a day. Should have never let himself be bewitched by her body at night. And he sure as hell couldn't let his mind conjure up their lovemaking. He'd go crazy.

* * *

Eustace Martin hurried as much as her tired body would allow up the last block to her house. With her mother gone, Mary was alone all day while she worked. A neighbor checked on the child, but Eustace worried still. She pulled her wool coat around her tightly as the wind snapped at her ears. Eustace came to a dead halt at the sight on her front porch.

"Mary. What are you doing outside in this weather, child? Miss Julia?" Eustace ran the last of the way.

"Eustace!" Julia cried and hugged her friend.

"Come on in. Open the door, Mary," Eustace said. "Let's get out of this cold."

"You told me, Mama, never let a stranger in the house," Mary said as they went into a small cozy kitchen.

"She did the right thing, Eustace. We were fine on the porch," Julia said as she unpinned the hat from her hair.

Eustace moved a kettle of water to a flame and tossed a log on the fire. "Mary. Start your school work for me while I speak to Miss Julia."

When Mary left the kitchen, Julia turned to Eustace with tears burning in her eyes. "I've never been so frightened in my life, Eustace. Or so miserable. Can I stay here with you awhile?"

Eustace gathered her friend in her arms. "Of course you can stay. Don't know what folks will say," Eustace held Julia away from her, "but we don't care none about that, now do we?"

Julia blubbered and cried until Eustace had heard the whole story. "So I'm here, alone, to get Jillian."

"I knew something was up when Mr. and Mrs. Crawford went out to see you. Your mother has had a sour look ever since I handed her your letter."

"That's why I can't stay there, Eustace." Julia dropped her head. "I'm terrified I'll just fall back into my old habits and end up never getting Jillian."

"How you plan on doing it? I sure hope you thought this out."

Julia looked at Eustace with grim resolve. "I'm going to tell Jillian before Mother does. Then I'm going to show the headmistress her birth certificate to prove I'm her mother. I'm going to write Aunt Mildred and see if we can stay with her for a while. Maybe look for a small house for Jillian and I nearby."

"You got enough money for all this? The traveling, a house, cooks and servants and all?"

"I don't need anything large, Eustace. Nor do I need servants. I don't have enough to live on indefinitely, but there must be something I can do to earn money."

Eustace cocked her head. "Miss Julia. I love you like you is my own daughter. But you never cooked and cleaned and such. Let alone get a job. Do you know what you're in for?"

Julia fingered her now soaked hanky. "Yes. As a matter of fact I do. I managed to keep Jake and I fed. Well, with his sister's help. And I cleaned the house and gathered corn at harvest. And I taught Millie and Danny. And, and . . ."

"I don't doubt for a minute you did all those things and did them just fine. But, well, Miss Jillian, she's used to fine things. Folks taking care of her and all. What do you think that youngin'll say about all this?"

"I don't know. I'm terrified she'll hate me."

"Now, now, Miss Jillian could never hate you. She loves you dearly."

Julia looked at Eustace and tried to stem the flow of tears. "Am I doing the right thing? Do you think I'm doing the right thing?"

Eustace looked away. "'Tain't for me to say, Miss Julia."

Julia watched as the woman's eyes darted everywhere but Julia's face. "Tell me Eustace. You're my oldest friend. Other than Flossie and Gloria, you're my only friend. Tell me."

"I'm just the charwoman, Miss Julia."

"You're more than the charwoman to me. Tell me," Julia whispered.

Eustace held Julia's hand and stroked. "I've been with your family for a lot of years now. I know how hard your mother and Miss Jolene made things for you. And I was right proud that you finally left to start on your own. But, Miss Jillian, I'm afraid, isn't going to see things the same. I'm thinking she'll not take this so well." Eustace hurried on to Julia's stricken face. "Now you asked me if I thought you was doing the right thing. The answer to that is yes. I think you're doing the right thing. Even now after all these years."

Julia's lip trembled. "You must have been so angry with me for letting mother run rough shod over me. Over my life. Over my daughter's life."

"Not mad at you. But ashamed of myself. I thought I was helping you, trying to nudge you on. Little bits at a time. Give ya some faith in yourself. I shoulda sat ya down years ago and told ya straight out there was no way to get what was rightfully yours without standing up to your mother. Weren't never right what she done. I

181

shoulda screamed and hollered till you up and stole Miss Jillian in the dead of night."

"I'm the one to be ashamed, Eustace. I've been hiding all these years from my mistakes. I'd still be hiding if not for Jake." Julia could barely speak. She had never felt this way about a man. Never thought she would. Their parting, his final words to her would haunt her till the day she died. She loved him so desperately. Julia swiped her cheeks. "Jake showed me a whole new way of living and thinking. He showed me love." She whispered, "And he hates me now."

"I don't believe it, Miss Julia. Don't believe it at all. This Mr. Shelling sounds like a fine man. A fine man indeed. Raising his sisters and all." Eustace stood and bustled around the kitchen. "I won't believe a fine man like that fell out of love. Chances of falling in are so rare; I don't believe a smart man like that don't still love you."

Julia shook her head and stared out the window. Voicing in a whisper, Julia repeated the most horrible portrayal of her Jake could have rendered. "He said he was glad I wasn't carrying his baby. That he didn't want me for his child's mother."

Chapter Fourteen

SUNDAY AT FLOSSIE'S FOR MILLIE'S birthday was dismal. The children questioned him relentlessly about when Julia was coming home. Will and Harry would not look at him square on, and Flossie and Gloria barely spoke to him. Jake had made Millie a miniature cradle for her rag doll. Millie fingered the carved wood.

"Thank you, Uncle Jake," she said quietly.

Jake picked the girl up and sat her on his lap. "What's the matter, sweet pea? Don't you like the cradle?"

Millie nodded and looked at him dejectedly. "I like it just fine, Uncle Jake. It's just that Aunt Julia was teaching me to say thank you in French. I wanted to say thank you in French like her."

"Silvo plat, or something like that, Millie. Stop your whining," Danny said.

"But I wanted to say it," Millie said. "When's she coming home?"

Jake picked up the ragged doll and stared at it. "I don't know that she's ever coming home."

Gloria harrumphed. Flossie muttered under her breath. He couldn't believe it. His own family had turned on him. He knew the reason things had been quiet all day, why no one would meet his eye. They blamed him for Julia leaving. Jake wasn't the one to abandon a child, and he shouldn't have to bear the responsibility for Julia's leave taking.

"What did you say, Flossie?" Jake asked.

Flossie banged a dirty pot in the sink. "Said who can blame her?"

Jake's ears were bright red and burning. He could feel his neck swelling and his veins bulging in his temples. "Fine thing to say. From my own sister, nonetheless," Jake said.

Harry and Will put coats on Millie and Danny and hurried them outside. Little Joshua was asleep in Flossie's bedroom. The kitchen was silent. Gloria clucked and puckered her lips. Flossie faced Jake head on.

"I have a few more things to say to you, too, Jake Shelling."

"Go on. Say your peace then. Get it out," Jake shouted.

"Oh, I intend to. I intend to, by God," Flossie said and slapped a spoon down on the table. "You're not always right. And you don't have the right to judge."

Jake stood and leaned over the kitchen table. "She left me, Flossie. First she gave up her own child to the same people that made her miserable all her life. Then she comes out here to hide from her shame. Marries me and then leaves faster than a jackrabbit."

"Do you think she wanted to leave her child, Jake? I know now why she cried every time she held Joshua," Gloria said. "She doesn't know any better. It's how she was raised."

"What do you mean how she was raised?" Jake asked.

"Julia's been held down by her mother all her life. Made to feel as though she was the ugly child, the fat child. You should have heard how she talked about herself to Gloria and I when she first came here. Said her sisters were the pretty ones. Why she wasn't married. You got eyes in your head, Jake. Julia's beautiful. What kind of ridicule did that girl carry to make her see herself that way? Then the first man that pays attention to her gets her pregnant." Flossie threw her hands in the air. "And the mother marries the man off to the virgin sister while Julia stands beside her."

"I can't imagine how horrible that was for her. At seventeen yet," Gloria added.

"Julia told me all that the night we got married. She seemed fine about it after she told me. Her parents visit upset her, that's for sure, but what's that got to do with all this?" Jake asked.

"Women don't think the same as men, Jake. We put more stock in what we look like than we probably should, but we do it anyway," Gloria said and plopped her head in her hand. "Look at me. Josh's three months old, and I'm still big as a barn. Will thinks I'm a big fat cow."

"Will doesn't think you're a big fat cow, Gloria. What a stupid thing to say," Jake said.

"I've lived with this scar on my face for ten years, Jake. Most times I don't even think about it anymore. Harry, well, Harry says he would never change one thing about me," Flossie said. "But when Julia's mother stared at me that day in the foyer, I felt like the first time you made me go into town after I got cut. Like everyone was staring. Like it was the only thing anybody could see."

"And the only thing Julia could hang on to was loving you and having your babies. Being worthy of you," Gloria said, tears on her lashes. "And you go and say what you said. Nothing could have hurt her worse."

"What are you two talking about?" Jake asked slack jawed. His sisters, capable farmwomen that they were had themselves in a tizzy about carrying baby fat and what some old Boston bitch thought of them. He was shocked.

"You're loyal and honest and would die for us, Jake. I know that. You're also stubborn and bull-headed and think your way's the only way," Flossie said hands on her hips. "And I know you were angry and shocked when you found out Julia has a daughter but to say you hoped she wasn't pregnant. That she wasn't worthy to have the children of the man she loves. My God, Jake. Nothing you could have said could have hurt that girl more. Nothing."

"She left her own flesh and blood there. Like she never had the girl," Jake said. "I can't imagine what would make a person do that. Things were hard in the beginning when Ma and Pa died. I would have never dreamed of leaving either of you."

"We know you wouldn't have, Jake," Gloria said. "But maybe Julia thought so little of herself that she thought she was doing the right thing? She was seventeen, Jake. Did you ever think that she loved the girl so much she thought life with her parents was better for Jillian than life with her?"

"Jake, it's hard for us to understand. I wouldn't do it. Gloria wouldn't do it. But by damn, it's not for you to judge her," Flossie said. "And she's not Valerie Morton. Right now, Julia's all alone in Boston, trying to set things right between her and her daughter."

Jake slumped down in a chair. He had not thought about Julia back with her family. No one would defend her there. "What did she say in her letter?"

"Said she was going home to Boston and get her daughter. Said she'd never forget the time she spent in our family. She didn't feel clumsy or stupid or ugly while she was here. But that she loved you more than anything besides Jillian, and she couldn't bear to live looking at your face everyday, knowing you thought so little of her. Julia said it was high time she started being responsible for herself and her daughter. And that she would have never understood any of it if it hadn't been for you. That she would be grateful to you to her dying day for forcing her to take a long hard look at her life."

Jake took a shaky breath.

Gloria unfolded the letter. *"I know what real love is now. I saw it in you and your sister's face. And for a brief, wonderful time saw it in Jake's. Tell him to get a divorce or whatever he wants to do."*

Jake stood slowly, feeling the weight of the passing years more heavily than ever before. He had some thinking to do. Some deciding to do. But there was one item not up for discussion or thought. "There'll be no divorce, damn it."

Flossie and Gloria eyed each other and then their brother.

"Well, right now Julia is facing that shrew of a mother of hers alone."

* * *

Julia dressed carefully for her trip to Ramsey. She and Eustace had talked endlessly about her strategy during her stay. No matter how much encouragement her friend offered, Julia began to realize the fact that Jillian may want nothing to do with her. Her plans, ten years in the coming, may fall irrevocably apart. There may be no cozy home and shared lives with a daughter she adored. Was it selfish to want to be with her daughter? Raise her? Dream for her and about her? Julia decided it might not be selfish to want those things for herself. But if her daughter rejected her, as Turner and Jake had, would she have the strength to keep trying.

"Giving up's the easy way, Miss Julia. Whatever happens, you can't give up," Eustace said to Julia the night before Julia's trip to Ramsey.

"I've taken the easy way all my life, Eustace. I just realized that," Julia said.

"No, no, Miss Julia. You did what you thought was right. What was right for that precious girl of yours."

"I used to think so. Not anymore. I was always looking for someone's approval. Someone that didn't care what I looked like or what mistakes I'd made. I had that in Jake. He never took the easy way all his life. Didn't care what people thought of him other than his family." Julia stood and walked to the sink in Eustace's kitchen to stare out the frosted window. "I've made my mistakes. I don't have anyone to blame other than myself. But I can't do the right thing now because of what Jake thinks. I'm alone in this, Eustace."

"You're not alone, child. I'm here. Your Aunt Mildred said you and the girl could come and stay for as long as you want or need. And a prayer or two probably wouldn't hurt none either."

Julia looked at the intricate pattern the ice made on the windowpane. "I'm terrified, Eustace."

"Go ahead. Be scared. I would be too. It's all right to be scared, Miss Julia. But don't let it stop you now. You've come too far to let that fear stop you."

Julia turned to Eustace. "I have come too far, Eustace. I can't quit now, can I?"

Eustace shook her head and smiled. "You left and got married. Come back and got your money from the bank. You're heading to see Miss Jillian tomorrow. One foot in front of the other is all you can do now, girl."

* * *

Julia clung to those words of encouragement as she climbed down from the carriage at the steps of the Ramsey School for Young Ladies. The slow march to the door of the brick building felt to Julia as though she were being led to an executioner. A prim matron answered.

"May I help you?"

"I would like to speak with Miss Abernathy if I may."

The woman tilted her head. "I don't believe the headmistress had any appointments for this morning."

If Julia could not get past this woman there was little hope. "I don't have an appointment. But I am a graduate of this school, and my sister attends currently. I was hoping to visit with her after chapel." The woman made a quick decision after eying Julia's most costly outfit.

"Come in and have a seat. I will see if Miss Abernathy can meet with you."

Julia sat on the velvet settee near the door. Her palms were sweating and her hands shaking by the time Miss Abernathy appeared.

"Miss Crawford. What a surprise," the tall thin woman said to Julia.

Julia had been terrified of the headmistress as a student. Her adherence to proper behavior made the Ramsey school sought after for their daughters by Boston's first families. Her unsmiling, unbending ways terrifying generation after generation of girls. Her belittlement of students she deemed unworthy, legendary. *I am no longer a child, Julia said to herself. I'm an adult.* The chant did not diminish the quiver in her voice.

"Good morning, Miss Abernathy. I was hoping to have a visit with Jillian this morning." The woman's lips disappeared in a smile.

"We do hate to disrupt the lives of our girls with unexpected visits. I'm sure you remember the rules, Miss Crawford. Your mother was here last week. She made an appointment."

Julia swallowed and repeated the well-rehearsed lines. "I do beg your forgiveness on that count. But I'm only here in Boston for one day. I'm sure a few moments with a sister is well within school rules." Julia smiled as pleasantly as possible. "*Family first* is the motto of Ramsey after all."

Miss Abernathy's brows raised and her lips pursed. "It is hardly necessary to remind me of our school motto. I have endeavored my entire life for the good of the school. As you well know."

Julia shook her head. "My goodness, I meant no disrespect, Miss Abernathy. I would never dream of being

191

so brash." Julia dropped her eyes. "I have spent my life living the lessons I've learned here." When Julia looked up, she saw the headmistress' smile of victory.

"We hope that for all our graduates." She tilted her head. "I suppose a few moments with your sister could do no harm." Miss Abernathy turned and began to stride down the hall. When she and Julia came to the door of a room, she turned. "Perhaps you can enlighten your Jillian on the importance of those lessons. She is undisciplined and headstrong. Humility is a trait needed for our young woman as they enter the world of marriage."

Julia was conversely elated to get through the gates of Abernathy and worried what censure Jillian had brought upon herself. And truly the moment of truth had come. She would face her daughter as a mother, momentarily. Miss Abernathy knocked briskly on the door.

"Miss Crawford. You have a visitor."

Jillian smiled brilliantly when she saw Julia. Had it not been for Miss Abernathy, Jillian may have responded with more excitement. As it was the girl cloaked her face in a mask and spoke softly.

"I am happy to see you, Julia."

Julia touched Jillian's chin and smiled. "I am so very happy to see you." Julia looked at Miss Abernathy as she watched the exchange.

"One hour, Miss Crawford." She turned to Jillian. "I certainly hope granting you this time will not interfere with your upcoming test."

Jillian's face hardened. "Thank you, Miss Abernathy. I will do my best."

When the door of Jillian's room closed behind them, Jillian threw herself into Julia's arms. "Oh, Julia. I've missed you so much. I hate it here. Miss Abernathy is a witch. The other girls are mean. I hate it here."

Julia hugged Jillian close to her and for so long, Jillian finally looked up at Julia with concern.

"Is everything all right, Julia? Are Mother and Father all right? Where is your husband?"

Tears misted Julia's eyes. She kissed the top of Jillian's head. "Everyone is fine, dear. Let's sit down here on the bed." Jillian eyed her curiously but sat down close and held Julia's hand. "I have something to tell you, Jillian. Something very important. But first let me ask you something."

Jillian jumped up. "I'm not going to that dreadful Elizabeth Bell's party. Mother sent you, didn't she? I won't go."

Julia shook her head. "This has nothing to do with Elizabeth Bell." Julia cleared her throat and handed out the first scolding she'd ever given. Mild as it was. "Don't call someone dreadful, Jillian."

Jillian drew her hands to the waist of her white eyelet dress. "I tell you I won't go. She's nasty. She doesn't like me, and she's a bore. Just because her father and Daddy know each other means nothing to me."

This was Julia's first view of her daughter without a cloud of guilt. It was not a pretty picture. "Jillian, I know nothing about Elizabeth Bell or her party." Julia swallowed and rubbed her sweating palms. "I've come to ask you if you'd like to leave Ramsey."

Jillian's eyes widened, and she nearly knocked Julia over with her hug. "Leave Ramsey? I would give anything, anything to leave this place. When shall we go?"

Jillian's smile tore through Julia. Julia's throat was dry and her stomach turned. "Remember I told you I had something to tell you?" Jillian nodded and scrambled down on all fours pulling a leather suitcase out from under the bed. "Jillian, sit here beside me. I need to talk to you."

Jillian clasped her hands in front of her chest and her blond hair swung in sheets around her shoulders. Eyes skyward. "You don't know how often I've dreamed of this moment." Jillian looked at Julia. Her eyes widened and she smiled. "Mother will be furious, Julia."

"Yes, I suppose she will. There should be no joy in making someone angry though, Jillian."

Jillian's head cocked. "You sound like Mother. Since you left, I'm the one taking the blame for everything. I can't tell you how glad I am you are home. What did your husband say about you leaving?" Jillian yanked open drawers and began to throw socks and undergarments in her now open bag. "He didn't care much, did he?"

Was the sweet girl of Julia's memory merely a figment of her imagination and longing? Or had Jillian always been this way, and Julia simply chose not to see it. She tried a tactic she'd seen Flossie employ. A stern look and voice seemed to settle Jake's niece and nephew in no time. "Jillian. Sit down. We need to talk."

Jillian sent her hairbrushes and toiletries into her suitcase in one wide sweep. "We can talk in the carriage, Julia." Jillian straightened. "You did bring the family carriage, didn't you? Nellie Mills goes home in this old thing Paul Revere must have rode in."

"Jillian, please sit down," Julia shouted. Jillian's head snapped up and her eyes widened. "I didn't mean to shout, but I need to talk to you about something very important."

Jillian acquiesced as she sat down beside Julia. "What is it, Julia?"

Julia swallowed hard and picked up Jillian's hand. She looked into Jillian's eyes. "There is no easy way for me to tell you, Jillian." Julia's lip quivered. "Mother is not actually your mother."

Jillian tilted her head. "What are you talking about, Julia. Of course she's my mother."

Julia shook her head and stared at the pale white delicate hand of her daughter. "No, Jillian. She's not. I am."

Jillian jumped from her place beside Julia. "That's not true. Father calls me his little girl. They sent me here like my sisters. Like you."

"Yes, they did. And don't doubt they care for you very much. But you are their granddaughter."

"That's a lie."

"I was very young, Jillian, when I had you. Mother," Julia swayed as her mother's voice revealing that long ago plan whirled in her head, "Mother decided it was best for everyone that you be raised as a daughter."

Tears filled Jillian's eyes. "Why are you doing this? Why are you saying these dreadful things?"

"Because it's the truth." Julia watched a mass mix of emotions play out on Jillian's face.

"You were not married, Julia." Jillian crumpled to the floor in a ball. "I'm a bastard, just like Mary Evans." She looked up at Julia with disgust. "No one speaks to her. It's only her father's money that keeps her here."

"Where did you hear such language? Young ladies don't say words like that."

"Don't be a goose, Julia. The girls here talk. We have older sisters and brothers. You think we don't know about things, but we do."

Jillian's tone was vengeful, derisive and filled with disgust. Julia had laden her daughter with a label she never expected the girl to understand. "We are not going to worry what the other girls say. We are leaving. You won't have to worry about any of this."

Jillian's eyes widened. "Does Mother know you are telling me this?"

"We are not returning to Market Street. I thought we'd visit Aunt Mildred for a while." Julia held her breath for Jillian's reaction. "We will stay at Eustace's tonight and then board . . ."

"Eustace's! She's colored!"

Julia stood up and glared at Jillian. "Eustace is my friend. She has been more of a friend to me than I can describe."

"She's a servant. I'll not stay there," Jillian said and crossed her arms over her chest.

Julia decided the time was not right for a confrontation. "Do you want to leave Ramsey?" Jillian's lip trembled as she nodded. "Then you will stay at Eustace's."

"I'm going home to Mother," Jillian spat. "She'll not make me stay with a nigger servant."

Julia's hand slapped Jillian's cheek before she could stop it. Mother and daughter stared at each other as Jillian's hand touched her face. This was surely not the time to back down. She and Jillian would have time later to sort everything out. For now, Julia needed to get Jillian away before her parents knew. "Mother will return you here in an instant."

Jillian slammed the lid of her suitcase closed and turned in a fury. "I hate you." Jillian pulled her coat off a hook and shoved her arms through the sleeves. "I hate you," she whispered as she stood at the door of her room, her back to Julia.

Julia's hands shook wildly. Her worst fears were materializing. She needed a chance to talk to Jillian when they had both settled down. She needed her heart to quit pounding and her knees to hold her upright. Julia needed the time to explain to her daughter why she done what she'd done and how sorry she was. She needed Jake.

Craved his arms around her. His encouragement to know she'd done the right thing no matter how ugly Jillian's reaction had been. Needed his conviction to keep what was hers, hers.

Julia and Jillian walked silently into Miss Abernathy's office past a sputtering assistant. Jillian followed. "This birth certificate indicates I am rightfully Jillian Crawford's mother. I am taking her home."

Miss Abernathy stood. "How dare you barge into my office? And what nonsense is this?" The woman took the paper from Julia's hands and read.

Julia watched the usually stoic woman as she read and came upon Julia's name as mother. Her eyes shot up. "This is ludicrous. You can't mean to take Jillian now. Your parents need to be notified."

"My attorney has researched the validity of this certificate. A duplicate is filed at city hall. As Jillian's mother, I am entitled to enroll or remove her from this school. It is merely a courtesy I extend to you by informing you."

Julia ushered Jillian out of the office as Miss Abernathy shouted her outrage. The two, mother and daughter, walked silently out the door and into the waiting coach. Jillian huddled on one side of carriage. Julia sat quietly reviewing all that had been said. Certainly, her start as a mother had been rocky. *One foot in front of the other, she chided herself.*

Chapter Fifteen

A DIVORCE, JAKE THOUGHT AND harrumphed as a he speared the last sardine in the can. His parents would have never divorced. He didn't know anyone who'd been divorced. But if Julia was gone for good, his dreams of children to pass his farm to were over. No use kidding himself, Jake thought. His time with Julia had led him far past a helpmate and someone to bury him. Her gee-gaws and painting and wall-papering were done with anticipation and an unspoken plan. Julia had prepared his home to be a place he wanted to spend time in and that children would be happy in.

All the little things his mother had done before she died flew through his head. Paper chains at Christmas. Cherry pies for the Fourth of July. Sharpened pencils in a tin can for his ciphering. All the little details he'd scoffed at that still burned in his memory. His children, if Julia and he had any, would remember doilies under lamps, paper dolls and a cozy room with a fireplace and rugs and throw pillows. Julia probably did all those things half-happy for their children to come and half-sad for the daughter who'd never enjoy it.

After a few days of self-imposed exile from his family, Jake had cooled off. He supposed Julia was doing exactly what she thought he would want her to do. And his reaction had been derision. Now, Jake couldn't shake the feeling Julia needed him. Like he needed her when Gloria had Joshua and the thought of his sister's death loomed before him. Or when she put on his old work clothes and rode out to the fields with Slim to gather corn. Julia took twice as long to pull errant ears from stocks and dropped them before she got to the wagon more often than not but that was hardly why he needed her that day. Julia stood side-by-side with him. Facing the kind of hard work she'd never experienced, trying to right a wrong her parents had instigated. He needed her courage that day.

And although it galled him to admit it, Jake needed her kisses and touches as much as he needed her body for sex. He was missing her eyes lighting up when he said he loved her. He was missing her saying it to him. Sleeping alone without Julia cuddled next to him, touching his face in the morning was proving to be more difficult than he'd expected. He'd slept alone for thirty-some years. But after six short months, he could hardly remember a day not waking up beside his beautiful wife.

Jake recalled Julia's exhausted but smiling face when she came home from Gloria's each evening after William's birth. He had kissed her nose and helped her take her shoes off one night. Jake had told her she was over doing, not used to doing laundry over a fire and scrubbing. Julia's face had glowed when she told him she was going back the next day. *They need me, Jake.* Nothing he had done or said to her had ever summoned that look on her face. She was proud as punch, and crying as usual, when she curled up that night beside him. And knowing her family, Julia probably needed him something terrible right now. Jake lowered the lamp. His eyes closed quickly, and he fell into the deepest sleep he'd had in weeks. Jake knew now, what he needed to do to keep what was his, his.

* * *

It took more than an hour for Julia to convince Jillian to come into Eustace's home. She was sure every eye in the neighborhood watched as they finally stepped out of the carriage. Julia had warned Jillian in the most serious voice she could summon; she would allow no disrespect of her friend or her daughter. Julia opened the door of the small home with the key Eustace had given her. Julia went straight to the kitchen to boil water for tea. Her nerves were frayed to their very ends. Jillian walked down the darkened hall, slowly, taking in all around her. The girl stood in the doorway of the kitchen, watching her mother.

"Why are you doing this to me?" Jillian said finally.

Julia pulled the hatpins from her hair. "Sit down. I'm going to change, and we'll have tea and talk."

After Julia had changed into one of her dark skirts and blouses, she found Jillian rooted to the same spot. "The kettle's whistling, Jillian."

Jillian just stared. Julia bustled around, finding teacups and opening a tin of sugar cookies.

Jillian repeated her question.

"I should have never agreed to Mother's plan. But I was seventeen at the time and thought I was doing the right thing." Julia took a deep breath. "I am so sorry."

"What if I don't want you for a mother?" Jillian asked. "You're always embarrassing us. Being silly and stupid. Jolene and Jennifer could hardly bear being at a party with you for fear of what you would say."

The words cut through Julia's heart. She hadn't realized how hurtful a ten-year-old could be. And she was now responsible for this particular ten-year-old. "Well, then, you'll just have a silly, stupid mother, I suppose."

"I don't want you as a mother."

Julia swallowed. "Well, I don't imagine you do. But unfortunately, you have nothing to do with who your mother is. We can't choose our parents, Jillian."

"No. You chose for me."

Julia refused to give in to tears. She opened the bag of flour from the groceries she'd bought for Eustace the day before. "I was wrong, terribly wrong."

"What are you doing?"

Julia looked up as she measured lard from a tin. "Making biscuits for dinner."

Jillian's brows rose. "You know how to make biscuits?"

Julia kneaded the dough in a crockery bowl. "I learned how to do lots of things while I lived in South Dakota. I gathered eggs and shucked corn. Flossie made all the bread for Jake and me, but I was tutoring Millie and Danny in exchange."

"Sounds dreadful to me," Jillian said as she plopped down in a chair. "Who's Flossie?"

"My husband's sister. And Millie and Danny are her children. Harry's her husband." Julia supposed until she was well and divorced she could still call Jake her husband." Julia sighed. "I loved it there."

Jillian harrumphed. "Yeah, away from Mother." The girls' cheeks reddened. "I'd still rather be home than here."

"We'll only be here for a day or so until we catch the train to Aunt Mildred's."

"I hate Aunt Mildred. She's a hundred years old, and she smells."

Julia cocked her head. "Aunt Mildred has graciously invited us to stay as long as we need. Until I figure out what I can do for an income."

"An income?"

Julia rolled out the dough on the wooden table. She did not look at Jillian when she replied. "I'll need to earn money. I have enough to get us started but not enough to live on indefinitely."

Jillian's mouth dropped. "Are you saying we're poor?"

"Not poor exactly. I believe I have enough to buy a small house with, but I'll have to do something to make money."

"And what could you do to earn us money. Mother said your husband would be lucky if you didn't burn his house down."

Julia bristled. "Mother would say that."

"It's true."

"Not anymore, Jillian, not anymore," Julia said. Her hands were shaking with anger. She'd gathered the courage to leave her home in Boston, to be away from ridicule; by damn she wouldn't live with it again. "Mother doesn't know everything, you know."

"Mother said your husband was sweet to you while she was there. She said it wouldn't last. She was right about that. I don't see him here," Jillian said.

Julia heard traces of Jolene and her mother in Jillian's tone. She would either bend to it or stop it. "What happened between my husband and me is private. He is certainly the reason I finally faced the mistakes I made in the past. I will forever be in his debt."

"I hate him for it."

Julia slammed down the wooden spoon in her hand. Jillian jumped. "I will not allow you to slander a man, a good, kind, honest man, you don't even know." Julia punched out the circles of dough with a vengeance. "The Shellings are the kind of people I always dreamed of for a family. Don't you dare judge what you don't yet understand."

Jillian sat silently while Julia placed the dough on a blackened pan. She cut ham into small chunks, potatoes as well and boiled them in water while she opened jars of beans. Julia was sweating and angry when Eustace walked in, Mary in tow.

Mary and Jillian eyed each other warily.

"Something smells mighty good," Eustace said as she pulled off her bonnet. "What a pleasure it is to see you, Miss Jillian. Mary, show Miss Jillian your doll collection."

"What doll collection?" Jillian asked warily.

Mary stood straight and met Jillian's look head on. "My mama makes dolls made of porcelain and she paints the faces. They're the most beautiful dolls in the world."

Julia glared at Jillian as she sat rooted in her chair. "Jillian, be gracious, please."

Jillian jumped up. "Fine. Can't imagine how beautiful dolls'd be made by a cleaning lady."

Julia shouted. "Jillian. Apologize this instant. You have one of Eustace's dolls in your room, and you always told me it was your favorite."

"Is not," the girl shouted, tears brimming in her eyes.

"You say you're sorry to my mama," Mary said.

Eustace took a deep breath and a step towards Jillian. "I was thinking about making gingerbread cookies tonight, Miss Jillian." She saw Jillian's lip tremble. "Now, I knows there your favorite. I made them the night before you left for . . ."

Jillian dissolved into pitiful sobs and launched herself into Eustace's arms. "I've missed you so much. I hated school, Eustace. Hated it."

Eustace stroked Jillian's hair. "I know you did, child. I know you did." Eustace looked at Julia's face over Jillian's head.

Julia ran from the kitchen and to the spare room she was staying in. She locked the door before the tears came. And then they came in torrents.

* * *

Eustace sat Jillian down and sent Mary to the neighbors for salt. "I think you've had a mighty hard day."

Jillian's sobs quieted and she hiccoughed. "Do you know? About me?"

Eustace nodded. "I knew before you was born, Miss Jillian."

Jillian's lip trembled. "Then why did everybody wait so long to tell me?" Jillian sat quietly and then faced Eustace. "My mother, the, the one I always thought was my mother can be, well," Jillian dipped her head, "mean. Julia always told me stories and took me to the park and hugged me. But she's my sister. Mother and Jolene said not to tell anyone at school who my sister was."

"So you're thinking you ought to be ashamed of her."

Jillian nodded. "But I . . . I don't know what to think, now."

"I think this is a lot of big changes for a little girl." Mary came in the kitchen door and eyed her mother and Jillian. "I think Miss Jillian would like to see your doll collection." Eustace hugged Jillian and whispered in her ear. "Don't think about anything right now, child. Just try and understand your Mama loves you and always has."

Jillian looked unconvinced but dutifully followed Mary.

Eustace didn't knock on Julia's door till much later. "Miss Julia?"

Julia dried her face and opened the door. Eustace followed her into the small attic room.

"Why don't you let Mary sleep up here? Then you can sleep in her bed. It's a nice, big room," Eustace said.

"I don't need a bigger room, Eustace," Julia said. "You've been more than hospitable already."

Eustace saw Julia's face and the dried tear tracks. "Now don't forget what I told you. One step at a time. You gave Miss Jillian lots to think about." Eustace stepped closer to Julia. "You knew this weren't gonna be easy."

Julia looked out the window as if looking for the answers eluding her. "She called you horrible names and was nasty to you." Julia faced Eustace. "Yet she came to you for comfort. I don't understand."

Eustace took Julia's hand and led her to the bed to sit down. "Now listen here. That girl is nasty just to cover up her own hurt. It ain't right, but that's all it is. She was mighty sad when you left to get married, then your Mama ships her off to that school, and you know what those high falutin' girls act like. Then you come home and tell her you is her Mama." Eustace grabbed Julia's hand. "Sure, she's mad. She's goin' say lots she don't mean till she sorts all this out."

"I know so little about children. I am surely out of my depths to be a mother."

"Nonsense, child. You'll learn. Ain't goin' to happen in one day, though."

Their evening meal was eaten in near silence. Julia was ashamed of Jillian's behavior and announced they'd be leaving the next day for Delaware. Eustace welcomed them to stay longer. Mary looked relieved. Jillian's face was a hard angry mask. She ate little, and Julia found her in their small attic bedroom, staring at the ceiling. She sat down on the low cot beside Jillian and rubbed her hand. "Won't you tell me what you're thinking?"

"I'm thinking I'd rather be dead than here."

"Don't say such things, Jillian."

Jillian rolled on her side to face the wall, pulling her hand unceremoniously from Julia's grasp. When Julia thought Jillian slept, she heard her low whisper.

"Why did you leave me?"

How could Julia explain? How could she describe the shame and fear she felt without making her daughter feel she was the cause? "Jillian, do you know how babies are made?"

"I'm not a baby, Julia. I know you're supposed to be married, cause then you sleep with your husband."

Julia's face colored even though her daughter did not face her. "A woman does not have to be married to get pregnant. It's an intimate act between a man and a woman. It should be between husband and wife, but it isn't always."

Jillian didn't respond but Julia continued. "What happened shouldn't have happened, but then I'd have never been blessed with you. I've spent years being ashamed and afraid. I know now my shame and fear are small compared to how much I love you. Through everything that happened I was never ashamed of you. Just myself. How I wish I'd not let Mother tell me what was best for my own daughter."

"But you did."

"And for that I am deeply sorry. I can't tell you how many times I wanted to explain it all to you. But I thought I was doing the right thing. When all along I was doing what Mother thought was best."

Jillian pulled the blanket over her shoulder. Julia lay down on the bed. Missing Jake. As she supposed she would for the rest of her life. The day had been an emotional nightmare. She needed him. Her daughter needed her more.

Chapter Sixteen

JULIA AWOKE AS THE WINTER sun filled the room. She dressed quickly in a navy traveling suit, shivering all the while. Jillian was already up. Julia took her time washing, knowing she had another long day of travel ahead. She didn't see Jillian as she entered the kitchen. There was a note from Eustace who had already gone to work at her parent's home. She had walked Mary to school before leaving. Eustace said her goodbyes and good luck in the letter. She promised that she would consider taking Julia up on her offer to live with her in Delaware once she was settled.

Julia looked around the kitchen wondering where Jillian was. She walked out to the small backyard to check the privy. No Jillian. She checked Mary's room, wondering if Julia had climbed into the girl's bed, although she doubted it. No Jillian. Julia's heart began a panicked beat to her throat. Julia ran to the front door and threw it open, expecting, hoping, praying, Jillian sat on the front porch. As she slowly closed the door and willed herself to remain calm, she saw the hooks by the front door. Jillian's coat was not there. Julia raced to the small room she'd been staying in. Jillian's shoes were not there.

Julia's hands were shaking and her knees weak by the time she sat down at Eustace's table and tried to clear her head and consider where Jillian may have gone. The girl would have never gone back to Ramsey. The only place Jillian could have gone, if she wasn't walking the streets of the city, was Market Street. The confrontation, Julia had hoped to avoid was now inevitable. Julia gathered her and Jillian's bags and sat them by the front door. She set off up the hill to an area busy with business and hailed a carriage. Julia had the driver take her back to Eustace's first to gather her things. She was amazed at how calm she was. As if there was no ugly scene yet to witness. Her hands trembled slightly in the cold air of the open buggy. There would be no Jake to stand between her and her parents. No hiding somewhere, whether it be in spinsterhood or fear or South Dakota. Julia would face her family alone.

It was near ten o'clock in the morning by the time the cabbie pulled up to the house on Market Street. She saw Turner's carriage and her father's as well. Everyone would want to be there, Julia thought to herself. See the fat, clumsy one humiliate herself one last time before finally admitting her inability to raise, even hold on to a ten-year-old girl. They would have a surprise.

Julia took a deep breath and looked up at the grand porch of her parents' home. She loved Jake desperately at that moment. Unwittingly he had given her the strength and the courage to face what would surely be ugly. She was no longer the embarrassment of this family. Nor the odd newcomer of Jake's family. Julia was a family of one. Soon to be three. Herself and her daughter and Jake's child. Nothing would stand in her way now.

Julia opened the door of her parent's home and lay her coat down over the velvet settee as if she had never left. Julia heard bits of conversation from behind the closed library doors. She went straight to Jillian's bedroom. Jennifer was holding Jillian in her arms as they sat together on the bed. They both looked up at once. "Julia!"

Julia marched to the side of the bed and stared at Jillian. Her heart was pounding. Her daughter was safe. Now wrapped up in a nightgown, under covers and safe. "You scared the life out of me, Jillian." Julia's lip trembled of its own volition. "Thank God, you're safe."

Jennifer stared at her older sister. "Is it true? What Jillian told me?"

"If she told you I'm her mother, it's true."

Jennifer nodded slowly. "That's what she told me."

"I don't want to live with Aunt Mildred. I don't want to be poor." Jillian sputtered between tears. "But Mother was so mad. I never saw her so angry when Eustace told her I'd followed her here. That I wasn't at Ramsey."

"Mother has little to say about this, Jillian. I told Miss Abernathy. You were there. I'm your mother, and I have the papers to prove it."

Jennifer slipped from the room.

Julia sat down beside Jillian. "I won't say I'm not angry with you. I am. Angry and afraid but I understand this has been overwhelming for you. It's been for me, too." Julia held her daughter's hand. "I have missed you so much, Jillian. I'm not leaving without you." Jillian looked up at Julia. "I know there's going to be some angry words when I go downstairs. I don't care. I'll stay as long as it takes for you to understand. I'm never, ever going anywhere without you again."

Jillian stared out the window. "Mother is so angry I left school." The girls' lip trembled. "She said she should have expected this behavior from me years ago. That the apple doesn't fall far from the tree."

"Never mind what your grandmother says."

"But you always made Mother angry and you would cry in your room for days. Now it will be me."

Julia took her daughter's face in her hand. "No, it won't. I won't let it be that way. We're going to go live with Aunt Mildred for a short while. We'll find a house. A school for you. Friends. It will be hard, but we'll be together."

"She says you'll never leave if you come here. That . . . . that you don't know what you want, and you'll soon be happy in your old room again," Jillian whispered.

Julia swallowed. How well her mother knew her. How much she'd changed. "I'll stay in a hotel until I can convince you to come with me. I won't stay here. If I have to get an attorney to get you, I will."

"You'd try to get Mother and Father thrown in jail?"

"No, but they will learn quickly, I won't back down. I intend to be your mother." Julia's voice shook. "And by God, if it takes until my dying breath, I will convince you to give me a chance."

Jillian lay back on her pillow. Julia rose and headed to the door. "I'm going to go speak to Mother and Father." She didn't doubt Jillian would resist but she intended to begin to set limits. "I would like you to get dressed and packed. We can still catch an evening train to Delaware."

Jillian watched her sister, her mother, sweep from the room. She was not the Julia of old. She rolled onto her side. Jillian had a lot of thinking to do.

* * *

Jennifer stood in the hallway and whispered as Julia emerged from Jillian's room. "Do Mother and Father know you're here?"

Julia shook her head. "How have you been Jennifer?"

"Fine, Julia," her sister said with wide eyes. "How have you been?"

Julia could not stop a smile at her sister's retort. "I'm doing well. I wrote to you. I don't know if Mother gave you my letters."

"She read them to us."

Julia rolled her eyes. "She read them in order to edit what she didn't want you to hear."

Jennifer stared at Julia but didn't deny her charge. "You've changed."

Julia smiled and straightened her shoulders. "Yes. Yes, I have. I loved it in South Dakota, Jennifer."

"Where's your husband?"

Julia's head dropped as she looked at her hands. No use hiding behind excuses any longer. She would rather Jennifer hear it from her than from their mother. "Home in South Dakota. When he found out I'd left a daughter, he made it clear I was not the wife for him."

"Oh," Jennifer said quietly. "It seems men can do what ever they please before marriage, and nothing's held against them. That's not true for us."

Julia smiled softly. "Jake could've cared less I wasn't a virgin." She continued to Jennifer's wide eyes, her voice cracking. "It was the fact I left my daughter in Mother's care that bothered him. He, he didn't think I'd make a fit mother for his children."

Jennifer grabbed Julia's hands. "You love him, don't you? Mother said you did, and that it would be your downfall."

"Jake's love will never be my downfall, Jennifer. Just the opposite in fact. Jake's love was the finest, most

215

wonderful thing to ever happen to me. He loves his family, his sisters and their families so desperately he just couldn't imagine why I'd done what I'd done." Julia shook her head and looked away. "I can no longer understand either. Yes, Jennifer, I love him. And he loved me."

"Jillian is very upset, Julia. I didn't know what to say. I had no idea either." Jennifer looked away and back at Julia with determination. "Why did you decide to come back?"

"Mother threatened to tell Jillian while she was at Ramsey. I know school was no hardship for you, but it was a nightmare for me and I think Jillian as well. If she would have told her when I was not there, I don't know what Jillian would have thought of me. Not that she thinks much of me now."

"I never cared much for Ramsey either, Julia. Jillian needs time to sort this all out. I do, too," Jennifer said. "What has Jolene in such a tizzy? Dragging Turner home from the office when Mother sent her a message about Jillian. She was red in the face and barking at William, ordering Turner around. That's when I came up here with Jillian."

No use sugar coating the family skeletons at this point. "Jolene insisted years ago that Jillian not be included in the division of the estate when Mother and Father were gone. She felt that if Jillian were, then any of her children should be as well. I imagine she's here to guard her inheritance."

Jennifer schooled her features as any well-trained Jane Crawford offspring could. Julia could not decide what her sister thought of Julia's speculation.

Moments passed till Jennifer spoke. "That would be Jolene's main concern, I imagine."

"Not to worry, Jennifer. Mother made it painfully clear when she visited that I would not receive my share if I did not come home. And I can't imagine this is the homecoming she was imaging," Julia said.

Jennifer's mouth dropped. "What will you do if you have no inheritance if you're not going back to your husband? How will you live?"

"I have a little over ten thousand dollars from Grandmother Crawford and the pin money father deposited that I never used. I had Mr. Flemming put it in a signature account. Would you like to see my passbook?"

"You went to see old man Flemming? What did he say?"

"He was none to happy. I told him I was entitled to the same conveniences and discretion as any depositor. When Jillian's ready, we're going to stay with Aunt Mildred until I can find a house for us. Won't you come visit?"

Tears filled Jennifer's eyes. "Oh, Julia. You've been so brave. Coming back for Jillian. Seeing Mr. Flemming. Facing Mother. I could never do what you've done. Ever."

Julia squeezed her sister's hand. "Yes you could, Jennifer." Julia tilted her head at the panicked look on Jennifer's face. "What is going on, Jennifer?"

Jennifer shook her head and dried her eyes. "Oh nothing. Other than Mother thinking that Horace Bradford is my future husband."

"Now, listen to me. You don't have to . . ." Julia stopped when she heard her mother's voice calling Jennifer.

"Has Jillian settled down, Jennifer?"

"You have to tell me, Julia," Jennifer whispered. "You must before Mother knows you're here. Who is Jillian's father?"

Julia looked her sister square on. "Our dear brother-in-law, Turner Crenshaw."

Julia thought certainly her sister would faint dead away. But Jennifer held her ground, and Julia watched the emotions on Jennifer's face change from shock to sympathy to horror before her eyes. Julia smiled and kissed her sister's cheek.

Jennifer's hand came to her face as she watched Julia walk to the top of the staircase and call down to the lion's den.

"Jillian will be fine, Mother."

"Julia!" Jane Crawford shouted. "What are you doing here?"

The library door swept open as Julia came down the steps. She met every gaze head on. Jolene's and her mother's distaste. Her father's shock. And Turner's embarrassment. "Let's talk in the library. Shall we?" Julia said as she walked among them to the open door of the library. "We wouldn't want the servants hearing any of this."

Although Julia kept her chin high, her heart shook. Never before had she seen her mother so angry. The hard lines of her face were near cracking. She followed Julia inside. William Crawford dropped into a chair. Turner leaned his arm on the mantle piece, looking outside. Jolene eyed her with a contempt so clear, Julia looked away. Her mother wasted no time going in for the kill.

"You don't actually think we'll allow you to take Jillian, do you? You couldn't hold on to her for the span of one day."

"Actually I do intend to take Jillian as soon as she agrees. And she will agree. I am her mother, after all," Julia said stiffly.

"You gave your rights up as a mother the day you walked out the door to South Dakota," Jolene spit out. "The most embarrassing thing you've pulled yet, Julia. Mother and I barely, and I mean barely, have people convinced you're still visiting relatives. Surely someone will see you here, and then what will we say?"

"I could care less what people think, Jolene," Julia said evenly. "And I gave up my rights; mistakenly, I might add, the day I agreed to Mother's outrageous plan, ten years ago. I am here to reclaim them."

"Julia, darling," her father began, "don't you see how uncomfortable this will make things for all of us? I want you to be happy, but you must know that but this wild plan of yours is just well, crazy. Jillian said you intended to live with Aunt Mildred and then buy a house."

"That's exactly what I intend," Julia replied. "And Father, although I imagine you did it unconsciously, the only person's happiness you were concerned about was Mother's. Otherwise she made your life a living hell."

Her father's jaw dropped. Jolene screamed about Julia's lack of respect and wit. Jane Crawford had yet to say a word.

"And what, pray tell, dear, do you intend to live on?" Jane Crawford smiled at Julia coldly. "A woman far past her prime with a child yet. No man will go near you."

Julia's lip trembled. "I'll find employment teaching or something. I have the inheritance Grandmother Crawford gave me to hold Jillian and I over until then."

"Teachers are always unmarried, dear. Chaste," Jane said.

"Then, then I'll find something." Julia could feel her resolve weakening in the face of her mother's manipulations. *Till my dying breath. . . One day at a time . .* Julia heard Flossie and Eustace's words in her head and squared her shoulders. "I'll scrub floors if I have to."

Jolene rolled her eyes. William Crawford leaned back in his seat and crossed his legs.

"Your daughter is accustomed to fine things, Julia. She'll not adjust easily and she'll blame you for her misfortune." Jane Crawford stared at Julia. "If you truly loved her, then you'd leave her here for your father and me to raise. If you truly loved her."

Jolene's eyes widened. "If she's entitled, then my William is entitled."

Jane Crawford turned an icy glare to her eldest. "Did I mention anything of an inheritance, Jolene? Raising her is an altogether different issue. In any case Turner will soon to be asked to run as lieutenant governor." She tilted her head and looked at Julia sympathetically. "I can hardly imagine you'd want to hurt his chances, would you? He's always had a special place in your heart, Julia, hasn't he?"

Six months ago, Julia would have acquiesced. Her mother's pleas for Jillian's love and Turner's appreciation would have been more than enough for Julia to agree to anything. Not so anymore. "He did once have a place in my heart," Julia said and stared at Turner. He looked at her red-faced and swallowed. "But not any longer."

Jane Crawford pulled the tight skirt of her silver silk gown under her as she sat down beside Julia. "No room in your heart, Julia? Your heart taken by another? Where is your farmer now, Julia?"

Chapter Seventeen

AKE'S TRIP ON THE TRAIN had been exhausting. He'd never been to a city as large as Boston and was glad he shoved a gun in his bag. It was teeming and crowded and smelled. And Julia was here somewhere, all alone. Jake towered over the other men shouting for carriages. He elbowed his way to the front of the line and climbed in the next one to stop over the roar of protests. Damn it all. Here he was, a long way from home in a city filled with suits and ties and poverty, and he barely understood why.

He didn't love Julia anymore, Jake had told Flossie. She'd laughed and then pointed out the obvious. *She's your wife, Jake. Love or not, are you going to let her face them alone?* And that was the only reason he was here, damn it all. *He didn't desert family. He didn't leave them alone in their* time of need. Jake reasoned he would help Julia get her daughter and take her back home. If he lived a loveless life, it was no more or less than he'd expected when he'd ordered Inga Crawper.

Jake had sat at Flossie's kitchen table yesterday morning telling her all the reasons he didn't love Julia. He missed her, he admitted, but that wasn't love. His sister had let him rant and rave without a word. Calmly. Flossie's demeanor scared Jake. When he finally ran out of words, Flossie just stared at him. He had to prompt her to speak her mind, something he'd never had to do before.

"Then why you going to Boston, Jake? Why go a thousand miles if you don't love her?"

It was the same question that had plagued him. The answer hadn't revealed itself in the sunset or the blank wall of his kitchen. A picture of Julia, frightened, facing her parents and that no good son of a bitch Turner Crenshaw came to mind. Julia didn't think of herself as strong or courageous. Jake knew better. But facing that crowd of jackals would scare anyone.

"She needs me, Floss."

Flossie stood and stuck a roast beef sandwich in his bag as if she'd anticipated his visit and plans. "Then get yourself to the train station."

* * *

223

Jake gave the driver the address Flossie had given him. The cabbie looked at the address than up and down at Jake. Jake fixed him the meanest scowl he could produce. The cabbie shrugged and yawed his horses. Jake looked down at himself. He was dressed just fine for anything in South Dakota. But he was wondering if his jeans and sheepskin jacket were right for a fancy house in Boston. Don't that beat all, he thought to himself as he straightened his string tie. Here he was worrying about how he looked. He didn't give a damn about how he looked. But he sure didn't want to embarrass Julia or her daughter.

Jake refused to let himself be cowed when the driver announced they'd arrived. He climbed out, all the while taking in the huge two story stone structure Julia called home. She must have thought his house was a hovel, like her mother had called it after having grown up here. It was a mansion, with trimmed gardens and a front porch longer than his bunkhouse, built to house twelve men. Julia fussed about his house like it was the finest thing she'd ever seen, painting and papering and fixing. Why, he wondered, as he walked up the gleaming painted steps.

A round black woman, rubbing her hands in an unconscious motion, answered the door. Her eyes darted to a door closed on her left as shouts resounded from within. "May I help you, sir?"

"I'm looking for my wife. Julia Crawford Shelling. Is she here?"

The maid's eyes rounded and she grabbed Jake's arm, pulling him inside and closing the door. "You must be Mr. Jake."

"Just Jake is fine. Are you my wife's friend, Eustace?"

"That I am, indeed, Mr. Jake. You gotta get in there with her."

Eustace pleaded with her eyes. The worry was clear in her words. "Is Jillian here, too?" Jake asked.

Eustace nodded. "Miss Jillian ran away from my house last night and come here. Miss Julia, she stayed with me, was going to take her to her Aunt's in Delaware but now, well, I don't know what's going to happen."

Jake patted the distraught woman's arm. "No need to worry over Julia. We're going home." Jake walked to the wide double doors and stopped, his hand on the knob when Eustace spoke.

"She doesn't think you love her no more. I told her a smart man like you would know a gem like her doesn't come along every day." Jake turned back to Eustace. "She loves you something awful."

The maid hurried to the back of the house as the shouting escalated. Jake heard Jane Crawford's shrill voice clearly. "Tell me Julia. Where is your farmer now?"

Jake pushed open the door of the room. "Had to catch a later train, Mrs. Crawford." His eyes found Julia in an instant.

Jake walked across the room staring at his wife. Her face was pale, and he saw her fingers twisting nervously in her lace hanky. His sweet, brave wife appeared as fragile as the clear glass figurine sitting on the table beside her. Jake knew she was strong, but the combination of forces in this room had her near shattering. Jake thought she was magnificent. Yellow hair and white skin against the dark velvet blue of her stand-up collar. He held out his hand to her as he stood behind her. She clasped it, and Jake felt the cold sweat of fear on her palm. He leaned down, kissed her cheek and whispered in her ear. "Where's Jillian?"

Julia's voice came out in a throaty whisper. "She's upstairs. I told her to pack."

Jake nodded and looked around the room. His head turned to the mannequin of a man in front of the fireplace as he spoke.

"What's the meaning of this?" Turner asked.

Jake's eyes darkened. This could only be the bastard responsible for Julia's predicament. "Who are you?"

Turner straightened his jacket. "I'm Turner Crenshaw III. What business do you have here? This is a family matter."

Jake took his time walking slowly to Crenshaw. He hooked his thumbs in his jacket and stared down at the lowly piece of shit now glancing nervously to his father-in-law. "Turner Crenshaw the third, huh. Mighty big handle." Jake looked Crenshaw up and down. "I'm Julia's husband. Everything that concerns her is my business."

"Julia is in over her head this time. She's spouting nonsense about raising Jillian and working as a washwoman." Turner gathered courage in his words. He looked Jake up and down. "Although that may suit a man like you."

Jake had promised himself as he rode the train to Boston he would not resort to violence. He broke his own vow in the next instant. Jake's hand snaked out, grabbed Crenshaw by his fancy silk tie and lifted him off the ground til he was eye-to-eye. "Don't you ever imply my wife's anything but a lady." He could feel everyone in the room jump to their feet. It didn't stop him from growling, "Especially you."

Turner Crenshaw fought for air and his dignity. "I had nothing to do with this."

Jake roared. "You had everything to do with it." He dropped Crenshaw unceremoniously and watched as the man stumbled to get his bearings. "You're the low down piece a shit that got her in this mess. Then turned around and married the sister."

Crenshaw's hand held his throat as he digested the words. He looked from Jane Crawford to Jolene to Julia. "They told me she had no idea who the father was," he whispered.

Jake's eye twitched and his fists clenched. "Are you saying my wife was with more than . . ." Recognition dawned in Jake. "They never told you, did they?"

"What are you implying, Shelling?" William Crawford shouted. "Just what are you implying?"

Jake turned his wrath on Julia's father. "You should have killed this son of a bitch. Or stuck a shotgun in his back til he married Julia. Instead you gave him another daughter." Jake could hear Julia crying softly. It was breaking his heart. He turned to Jane Crawford and her daughter, Jolene, sitting side by side. "You never told them."

"There was no cause," Jane Crawford said. "We had no idea which man it might have been. Certainly no use in causing any disruption to a very successful match."

Julia jumped from her seat, tears streaming down her face. "I told you. I told you both. I'd never been with anyone other than Turner," she screamed.

Turner Crenshaw and William Crawford stared open-mouthed at their wives. Jolene looked away.

"Julia would've never been able to take advantage of the opportunities I knew Turner presented. Jolene was the better-suited partner," Jane Crawford said.

Suddenly Jake needed to be far away. He wanted no parts of this sick scheme. He reached Julia as she stumbled back to her chair. Jake picked her up and looked around the room. William Crawford stared at him. "Get our daughter. She's coming with us right now. I don't want Jillian in this house for one more instant," Jake said.

"She's not your daughter," Crenshaw whispered. "She's mine."

Jolene shook her head. "Really, Turner. Exactly how would we explain that away?"

"She's got your balls twisted in one grand knot there, Turner," Jake said.

Julia was weeping against his shoulder when he realized a young girl stood in the open doorway of the library holding another woman's hand.

"Jillian?" The stunningly beautiful child nodded. "Are your things packed?" She nodded again, and he smiled. "Good girl. You're going home with your mother and me. I'm your father now. We've a long train ride ahead of us." Jake walked calmly to Jillian. "Your mother's all tuckered out. Stick your hand in my pocket so I don't lose you."

Jake looked at the young girl as she scanned the room. Indecision, fear and a multitude of other emotions Jake had no idea of. "This is your mother. I'm your father. I live on a big farm in South Dakota. You have two, no, now three cousins waiting to meet you. Plus two aunts and two uncles."

* * *

Jillian stared up at the giant telling her he was her father. He was holding Julia tight and kissed her forehead. Her mother, no, her grandmother, was red in the face, and her stare bored into Jillian's stomach. Jolene sat quietly as if no one was shouting. Her father was pouring whiskey in a glass. Turner was looking at her with the strangest expression. Julia was going with the giant that she was sure of. Jillian didn't understand all that was said when Jennifer opened the library door, but Jillian knew it was bad. And it was about her. She glanced back up at the giant. He smiled and held Julia as if he had all the time in the world. Jillian stuck her hand in the soft fur-lined pocket of the giant's coat.

* * *

Jake sighed with relief. He didn't want to stay in this house, in this town one more minute than he had to. But he figured he needed to give the girl a little time to get comfortable considering the ugly scene now erupting around him.

"I'll have my attorney after you," William Crawford shouted.

"Jillian," Jane Crawford said. The girl stopped and looked over her shoulder. "If you go out that door, don't expect to come back. There will be no fine clothes and carriages. No opportunities like your father and I can give you."

"I'm going to go live with Julia and her new husband, Mother."

Jake knew Julia heard what Jillian had said. Her cries renewed, and she was shaking all over. She hadn't lifted her head from his chest, though. "Come on then, Jillian. I've got a buggy out front, and we've got a train to catch."

"Won't you come visit, Jennifer?" Jillian asked. Jennifer nodded and swiped at her cheeks.

Eustace handed Jillian her black leather bag and motioned Tom to carry the trunk to the waiting carriage. "You take good care of your mother, girl, you hear?"

Jillian hugged Eustace. "I will. And tell Mary I like the dolls you made. I've got mine packed in my trunk." She stuck her hand back in Jake's pocket and led the way out the door.

Chapter Eighteen

J AKE CARRIED JULIA DOWN THE steps to a waiting carriage. She felt blissfully safe in his arms, smelling his scent. He was dressed up in his best shirt and string tie. Julia touched his chest.

"Put me down Jake. I can walk from here," she said. He was staring at her expectantly and Jillian still had her hand in his pocket. She'd never been so grateful as when her husband walked into her parent's home. "Thank you, Jake. I could never repay you for coming all the way from home and putting yourself in the middle of that horrid scene."

"You're my wife, Julia," Jake said. "I wouldn't have been able to live with myself knowing you were facing them all alone. Come on now. Let's see if we can make it back to the station in time to catch the evening train back home."

Julia looked at the house of her youth. She pictured Jake's house with its red front door. She had come and gone so very far from both. As much as she wanted to put her hand in his and step into the waiting carriage, she could not.

Julia was done with tears and self-pity. She was her own woman with a child to raise and another one on the way, and she could not live her life on someone else's terms any longer. How could she look the man she loved in the eye, everyday, knowing he didn't think she was fit to be a mother? How could she live with Jake, loving him as she did, knowing that he didn't love her?

"Jillian and I will be catching the train to Delaware. I'm not sure when a western bound train will be leaving."

"You're both coming home with me," Jake said. "Now get in the wagon."

"No, Jake, we're not," Julia said. "My Aunt Mildred has offered Jillian and I a home until I find something for us."

"You've got to be funning me," Jake said. "This is the Aunt that lives in Delaware?"

"I wouldn't make light about something this serious," Julia said.

"What are you going to do to support yourself?" Jake asked.

"I'm not a child, Jake Crawford," Julia said. "I came here on my own, got Jillian on my own and intend to continue with my plans."

Jake yanked his hat from his head and slapped it on his leg. "Damn it all, Julia. Are you waiting for me to say I want you to come home? I want you to come home. Are you waiting for me to say I'll raise this child here as if she were my own, guard her as if she were my own? She was my daughter from the day I married you, Julia."

"I'm not waiting for or expecting anything," Julia said. "You're welcome to share the carriage with us if you'd like. Get in please, Jillian."

Julia climbed in behind her daughter, settled her skirts and looked at Jake. "The Delaware train is due to pull out in less than an hour Jake. I'd rather not stay the night in a hotel."

* * *

Jake climbed into the carriage and wedged himself beside Julia. He shouted to the driver and turned in the seat to face his wife. "I'll be damned if you're not coming home with me. When did you get this crazy idea in your head you were moving to Delaware?"

"Perhaps when you told me you were glad I wasn't expecting. Maybe when I realized what a mess I've made of my life," Julia said.

"You haven't made a mess of your life, Julia," Jake said. "I never said that."

"And the other Jake?" Julia said. "Do you deny it?"

"No. I don't deny it. I was mad, Julia. Furious you'd lied to me. I still don't understand it," Jake said.

"Then I think it's best I continue with my original plans," Julia said. "At least for now. You and I both need time to sort out what we think."

"Your original plans were to move to South Dakota and get married," Jake said. "And marriage means for better or for worse."

"I don't want to live with Aunt Mildred," Jillian said.

"Children need a mother and a father, Julia," Jake said.

The carriage pulled up at the train station and Julia and Jillian gathered their bags while a porter loaded their trunks onto a cart and Jake paid the driver. Julia read the chalk board signs and found the platform the south bound train would be leaving from. The crush of passengers and the smell of hot metal against metal assaulted Julia's senses and reminded her of another train she'd disembarked from over six months ago. The conductor helped Jillian onto the step; and Julia turned to Jake.

"They need a mother and father that love each other enough to forgive each other," Julia said and pressed a note with her aunt's address scribbled on it into Jake's hand. "I don't think you can forgive me, Jake. I never wanted to lie to you. But I'd never met anyone like your family before. So giving and kind. I love you more than life, Jake, but I'm not certain you love me."

Jake was staring at her and she took in every detail of him possible. Tall and strong and handsome. Kind and gentle and hardheaded. She loved him so desperately.

"But I won't ever keep something from you either," Julia said and took a deep breath. The whistle was blowing, and the conductor was motioning for her to board the train. "I'll be having a baby late next summer."

Julia reached up, kissed Jake's cheek, grabbed Jillian's hands and turned and boarded her train.

* * *

Jake stood at the edge of the train platform till Julia's train was long gone and another one had pulled in it's place. Passengers were bumping him as they queued up to board and for his life, Jake couldn't get his feet to move. For a fleeting moment he considered boarding the train in front of him. It didn't really matter where he went. His family had left him.

But two long, dirty days later he pulled into the station at Cedar Ridge. Jake got his horse from the livery stable and rode home. The winter wind was biting at his face and his hands were near numb when he topped the ridge only a quarter mile from his spread. The first thing he spied through the blowing snow was a red front door. And Jake couldn't kid himself any longer that the tears on his cheeks were just from the wind in his eyes.

* * *

Julia and Jillian's train pulled in late in the evening to Newark, Delaware. Jillian was long asleep on her shoulder. Julia, however, did not sleep a wink. Every time she closed her eyes, she envisioned Jake's face. The station master found them transportation and Julia finally stepped onto the porch of her Aunt's home near eleven o'clock at night.

Aunt Mildred's butler, Richard, cracked open the front door, dressed in his nightshirt and cap.

"Miss Julia!" Richard said. "Come in!"

"Who is it Richard, at this ungodly hour," Julia heard from behind the butler.

"It's Miss Julia, Mrs. Delacroix," Richard said.

"Julia! Heavens to mercy, leave her in," Aunt Mildred said as the door opened wide. "And your sister, Jillian, too. Well, I declare."

Julia let herself be enveloped in Aunt Mildred arms.

"I'm so sorry I didn't give you any notice of my arrival," Julia said.

"As if I cared. No. Not one little bit," Aunt Mildred said.

"I'm not her sister," Jillian said. "I'm her daughter."

Aunt Mildred kissed the girls' head and looked up at Julia. "Is that right, dear? You're a very lucky young lady then."

Richard carried their bags and Jillian followed the butler up the wide staircase. Julia and Mildred climbed the steps arm-in-arm.

"I can only imagine you've had an interesting visit in Boston, dear," Aunt Mildred said with a chuckle. "Jane must be in quite a state. Jolene, as well."

"It was horrible, Aunt," Julia said. "Truly horrible."

"Well, it's all done now. Truth always wins out," Mildred said and kissed Julia's cheek. "Get some sleep, dear, and we'll hash it out in the morning."

Jillian climbed into bed and was soon asleep. Julia lay beside her and stroked her hair and face. She touched her stomach and thought about the day when Jillian would have a sister or a brother.

* * *

The sun streamed in Julia's room and she woke with a stretch and a yawn. Jillian was on her stomach, eyes closed and breathing softly. Julia dressed, washed and found her Aunt in the breakfast room at a table tucked in a window nook.

"Here you are! You were never up until ten in the morning if I remember correctly. This must seem quite early to you," Aunt Mildred said.

"I got used to getting up early when I was living in South Dakota," Julia said as she poured herself a cup of tea.

"Jane did tell me you were living in the wilderness," Aunt Mildred said with a smile. "Tell me about your husband. Your Mother dislikes him which makes me certain I would adore him."

Julia told her aunt everything that had happened in the last six months. When she was finally recalling the events of the previous day, Mildred inched closer and held Julia's hand.

"Your mother said that? She actually said she wasn't sure who Jillian's father was? My God. Jane's gone too far this time. And Turner had no idea. I always wondered if they ever told him," Mildred said.

"It was the most dreadful scene," Julia said and closed her eyes. "Then Jake came."

"And he handled those villains, didn't he?" Mildred asked.

Julia nodded and her lip trembled. "He shook Turner by the neck, and then he picked me up and carried me out of the house."

Mildred clasped her hands under her chin. "How marvelous! I've got to meet him. Where is he? Is he on his way?"

Julia shook her head and tears threatened. "When he read Mother's letter and found out about Jillian, he said he was glad I wasn't expecting. He said he didn't want any child of his to suffer like Jillian. He was so angry."

"That was a stupid thing to say. Why I'm sure you're going to be a wonderful mother now that you're free to do so. Did he apologize?" Mildred asked.

"No. And now I am expecting. I can't look him in the eye," Julia said. "I love him so very much."

"Does he know he's going to be a father?" Mildred asked.

Julia nodded. "I told him just as I got on the train."

"Well, well, well," Mildred said. "What a fix you two have gotten yourselves into now."

"Should I have gone with him?" Julia asked.

Mildred poured herself more tea. "No, I don't think so, dear. I think more than anything you need some time alone to lick your wounds and sort out the last few months."

"I've been such a child, Aunt Mildred," Julia said. "Why I ever waited this long to claim Jillian is suddenly inconceivable. Maybe Jake's right."

"I can only imagine what daily living with my nephew's wife is really like. Jane can be quite forceful. And don't scold yourself now. It's over. You're a grown woman, Julia Shelling," Mildred said. "What's done is done."

* * *

Jake was sitting at his kitchen table drinking coffee when the back door opened and Flossie came in his kitchen. He had spent the last evening and nearly the whole morning thinking about what he was going to do about Julia. He could have kicked himself for being so high-handed in Boston. He should have apologized but he was so damn mad at her family for hurting her the way they did, he couldn't see straight. If she wanted to go to Delaware then he should have taken her there instead of arguing with her. But all he could think about was home. It had taken a two day train ride to realize home was where Julia was, wherever that was. On their ranch, in Delaware, it didn't really matter.

"Jake," she said. "Where's Julia?"

"Glad to be home, sis," he replied and stood to pour more coffee in his mug. "Thanks for asking."

Flossie unwrapped the scarf from around her neck and stamped her boots. "Don't tell me you didn't bring her home."

"She didn't want to come home, Flossie," Jake said.

"Where'd she go?" Flossie asked.

"Delaware," Jake said.

Flossie poured herself a cup of coffee and sat down and waited. "What happened, Jake?"

"You should have heard the things they were saying to her," Jake said. "That her sister was the 'better suited' partner for that low sack of shit that's her brother-in-law. That they didn't know who Jillian belonged to anyway."

Flossie's eyes rounded. "Oh my God, Jake. What did Julia say?"

Jake wiped his eyes on his sleeve. "She was shaking all over. Thought she'd fall down when she got out of her chair. But her chin was up. She didn't back down an inch. Not an inch."

The kitchen was quiet other than the sound of Jake's breathing and the clock ticking on the mantel in the living room. The picture of Julia facing her family floated through his consciousness. But the vision that held him was of his wife at the train station when she kissed his cheek.

"Julia's expecting," he said. He looked at Flossie. "I'm going to be a daddy twice over."

"Ah, Jake," Flossie said. "I'm so glad for you."

"The thing is Julia's still got it in her head what I said about her not being a good mother. She's going to be a great mother," Jake said.

Flossie smiled. "Don't tell me, Jake Shelling. Tell your wife."

Jake nodded. "I think you and Gloria were right. I don't think I could have hurt her worse than saying what I said. She already thought she was doing a lousy job of it, and I go on and say what I did. Then I go and let my pride and being mad get in the way of saying I'm sorry. I don't know what to say to her, Flossie."

"Start with 'I'm sorry'," Flossie said and stood and pulled her coat on.

"I don't know that'll be enough," Jake said.

"Give her a little while, Jake," Flossie said as she leaned down and kissed her brother's cheek. "Give her a little time."

Jake started a letter to Julia ten times over. Everyone he balled up and threw in the fire. What he needed to say, he needed to say face-to-face with his wife.

* * *

"No. I won't apologize," Jillian shouted at Julia. "I don't want to live here."

Julia rose from her seat at Mildred's dining room table. "Follow me, Jillian," she said as she rounded the table and headed to the staircase. She waited at the door of her room for five minutes for Jillian to appear. She motioned her daughter inside and closed the door.

"I will not have you speaking to Aunt Mildred that way, Jillian," Julia said. "Would you like to stay here in your room while I finish my supper? Because you're not coming back to the table until you apologize."

"I hate you," Jillian said. She ran past Julia and threw herself across the bed.

Julia sat down on the bed beside Jillian. "I don't hate you. I could never hate you. I may be disappointed in what you do or say, but I'll never, ever hate you."

Jillian turned her head to see Julia's face. "Ever?"

"Never," Julia said and shook her head. "I know this has been difficult for you. But it will get better. I promise."

"What if Mother comes for me? She always treated me different, and Jolene hated me," she said.

Julia sat back on the bed and pulled Jillian into her arms. "It doesn't matter what Mother does. You're staying with me. And I don't imagine your Aunt Jolene will be visiting, so it won't matter what she thinks of you."

"I liked Jake," Jillian said. "Doesn't he like me either?"

243

Julia kissed her daughter's head. "He loves you," she said.

"How would he love me? He doesn't even know me," Jillian said.

"He loves you because he loves me," Julia said and fought the tears welling in her eyes.

"Then if you love him, why are we living at Aunt Mildred's?" she asked.

* * *

It had been a little over a week since their arrival in Delaware, and Julia had spent the days in the garden, reading with Jillian or just talking about everyday things. Jillian was quiet but seemed less wary and angry. She had even played checkers with Mildred one evening.

"I win!" Jillian said.

"Yes, you did," Aunt Mildred said. "Again."

"It's bedtime now, Jillian," Julia said. She pushed her needle through the fabric of her needlepoint. "Winifred will help you change." Jillian kissed Julia's cheek.

"Good night. Good night, Aunt Mildred," Jillian said.

"Well," Mildred said as the door to the drawing room closed. "That was done with less hysterics than other evenings."

"She has been a trial," Julia said. "But she seems to be settling in finally."

"And you, Julia? Are you settling in?" Aunt Mildred asked.

"We've imposed long enough, haven't we?" Julia said.

"That is not what I meant, Julia," Aunt Mildred said with a smile. "You know you may stay as long as you like. I've enjoyed having you immensely and will miss you and Jillian both when you go."

"I suppose I should begin house hunting," Julia said. She dropped her needle work in her lap and sighed. "But I manage to find a reason to put it off day after day."

Mildred folded the checker board and sat back in her chair. "I wonder if it's because you already have a house. A home as well. Just not here in Delaware."

Julia envisioned her sister-in-laws at her kitchen table and her sitting room with it's new wallpaper and acres and acres of corn. "I miss it dreadfully. I miss Flossie and Gloria and the children. I miss everything and everyone."

"And your husband? I'm sure you miss him as well," Mildred said.

Julia closed her eyes. Jake's face was before her as if she could reach out and touch him. Swinging her around in a great bear hug when he came home for his supper. Listening to her plans with the house. As she left him at the train station, holding his hat and staring at her.

"I didn't know anything could hurt as much as this," Julia said. "I miss him desperately. I told Jillian he still loves me. It came out without thought. As if I know it but won't admit it. Or maybe just wish it."

Mildred rose and sat down beside Julia on the settee. She picked up Julia's hand and squeezed. "Then go, Julia. Don't leave one of life's rare chances go by the wayside for fear of failure or hurt pride or anger or anything else. Tell him you love him. Tell him you miss him. It doesn't matter any longer why you were angry. It doesn't matter what your mother says or does any longer. None of it matters. Be honest with yourself and with him. Regardless of what you think he might do or say. Do it and say it for you."

* * *

Julia lay in bed long after she heard the last creek of a floor board. The night moon was shining and Julia wondered if Jake was staring at that same moon. Did she care any longer that Jake had read her letter? Could he ever forgive her for her deceit? Would he have said he was sorry for hurting her if she'd given him the opportunity? Did it matter who was sorry first or most? She would never know the answer to any of it as long as she was in Delaware. She had things to say to her husband.

* * *

Julia packed the last of things in her trunk and stood up to stretch her back. She pinned her hat in her hair and rang for Richard to carry her things. She and Jillian were catching the train to South Dakota that morning. She was nearly at the last step when Mildred's doorbell rang.

"Just set my things anywhere, Richard," Julia said. "That's probably Aunt Mildred's company. Although it is quite early."

Jillian and Mildred walked in to the foyer hand in hand and Jillian was clutching the velvet box that the girl had so much coveted during her stay. Richard was opening the door and Julia smiled at Mildred. "What do you say, dear?" Julia said to her daughter.

"I'm sorry," came a familiar voice from the threshold. "I'm sorry Julia."

"Jake!" Julia said as she turned. Jake was standing just inside the doorway, twirling his hat in his hand.

"I should have never read that letter from your mother, let alone judge you for what you did. I should have come with you to Delaware if that's what you wanted. I was just so damn angry at the things your mother said, I couldn't think straight or see it from your point of view. I'm sorry, Julia. For all of it."

Jake looked down at the luggage on the floor and back to Julia.

"Did you find a house?" Jake asked. "Are you going there today?"

Julia's lip trembled. "Oh yes, Jake. I found a house. I am going there this morning." She walked slowly to her husband. "It has a red front door and acres of corn, and I miss it something awful."

Epilogue

JULIA DIDN'T THINK ANYTHING COULD have looked quite as good as her little house in South Dakota. Jake had just carried her trunk to their bedroom. Julia pulled her hat from her head and watched Jillian as she looked around.

"It's nothing like the house in Boston," Julia said. "But it's ours."

"Do I have a room?" Jillian asked.

"You sure do," Jake said as he came into the kitchen. "Your Aunt Gloria's old bedroom. You'll have to get to town and pick out some new paint. I imagine your mother will be wanting to fuss over it, and we've got some Christmas presents to buy."

"For who?" Jillian plopped down in a chair. "Can I pick the color?"

"Yeah, you can. You and I will be doing the painting too."

Julia was heating water on the stove. "I'll paint it, Jake. I don't mind."

"Oh, no, you won't, Julia," Jake said. "You're expecting, and I won't have you doing anything more than putting on your stockings."

"Don't be silly Jake," Julia said. She watched her husband's face. He had the same look as he did when she'd gone out that day to pick corn. He was trying desperately to not shout. Julia smiled. "Fine, Jake. If you don't want me painting, I won't paint."

Julia turned when the door opened. Flossie, Harry, Danny and Millie came in with a whirl of winter wind. Millie ran straight at Julia, and she picked up her niece and swung her around in the air. "I missed you," Julia said. Danny was smiling up at her and she bent down and kissed his hair. "I missed you, too."

"We missed our French lessons, Aunt Julia," Danny said.

"Give your Aunt a minute to catch her breath. She doesn't even have her coat off," Flossie said. "Harry saw your wagon coming over the rise, and I couldn't wait one more second to meet my new niece."

Flossie held her hands to her face when she looked at Jillian. "Dear Lord! What a little beauty. Your cousins are about dying to meet you. This is Danny, and that one jumping up and down is Millie. Your Uncle Harry's the one dragging snow in on your mother's clean floor."

Jillian laughed.

"Well, what do you think?" Flossie asked. "Do you like it here so far?"

Jillian shrugged. "I don't know yet. This place is a long way from town. What do you do all day?"

The back door opened again and in came Gloria and Will carrying the baby.

"Joshua," Julia said. "Let me see him." Gloria kissed her cheek, and Will handed over the baby. Julia cuddled the newborn and kissed his downy hair. "He's gotten so big."

"Where's my new niece?" Gloria said. She wrapped her arms around Jillian. "We've been waiting forever to meet you."

Jillian submitted to Gloria's hugs and said a quick yes when asked if she wanted to hold the baby. She was seated at the table with Millie and Danny on each side of her.

"Why don't you come home with me this afternoon, Jillian? I'll show you some of the things we do all day. We've got to get dinner ready for ten. I could use the help," Flossie said.

"Ten?" Jillian said.

"I figured I'd cook tonight since your mother wouldn't have time to get anything started," Flossie said and leaned close to Jillian. "Millie and Danny are too young, but I'll bet you're a big help."

"I guess I could," Jillian said. "Mother? Can I go to Aunt Flossie's? She needs help with dinner."

Julia nodded. She would cry if she spoke. Jillian had called her Mother. Jake ambled over and wrapped an arm around her shoulder.

"That's fine, Jillian," Jake said. "Your mother and I will be over close to supper time." Jake looked at Flossie. "Best get going then. The snow's really coming down. And I want to get home early. I don't want Julia getting over tired, and Jillian's got a long day ahead of her tomorrow."

"What am I doing tomorrow?" Jillian asked.

"Slim picked out a pony for you. You've got to see to its stall and food," Jake said.

Jillian's eyes lit up. "A pony. Of my own?"

"Can't have you living in South Dakota and not be able to ride," Jake said with a smile. "Everybody best get going."

"Jake!" Julia said.

"We'll see them in an hour or two," Jake said.

Harry and Will were snickering. Gloria and Flossie pulled on their coats.

"Bye, Flossie. We'll be there for supper," Jake said as he closed the door on his sister with a bang.

"Dear Lord, Jake," Julia said. "You nearly slammed the door in her face."

Jake was taking the stairs two at a time, dragging Julia by the hand as he went. He pulled her into their bedroom and kissed her till her knees went weak.

"We haven't had two minutes alone together," Jake said as he stripped off his shirt. He wrapped his arms around her. "I've got some things to say to you, and I'd prefer to say them when we're both in bed."

"Jake!" Julia said with a laugh.

Jake dropped his pants and stepped out of them. He pulled back the sheets and climbed into bed and rolled onto his side. "Get naked for me, darling."

Jake's eyes were dark as coal and he watched her every move as she pulled off her jacket and unbuttoned her skirt. She put one foot on the edge of the bed and rolled down her stocking. Jake licked his lips. Julia pulled the ribbon from her hair and dropped the straps of her chemise. She climbed in bed beside her husband.

Jake ran his hand down her side and pulled her hand to his mouth. He kissed her fingertips and touched her face and hair.

"What is it that we've got to be naked for you to say, Jake?" Julia asked. She touched the coarse hair and the bulging muscles of his chest.

"You are the most beautiful woman I have ever seen, Julia Shelling," Jake said. He rolled onto one elbow and loomed over her cupping her cheek with his hand. "I said and did some pretty stupid things over the last month. I hope you can forgive me. I love you, Julia. I'll always love you."

Tears rolled down the side of Julia's face and into her hair. "I don't ever want to be apart from you or Jillian again. I'm sorry I left without telling you. I love you so very much." She reached up and kissed her husband's lips softly. "I love you for making me go to Boston and coming for me there. I love you because you're the best father a ten-year-old could ever dream of. I'm so glad I married the wrong man."

Jake rolled onto his back and pulled Julia atop of him. He held the back of her head, kissed her hard and let his loose hand wander up and down the length of her. Jake slid inside her with a groan. "It's been a while, Mrs. Shelling. I don't know if I can . . ."

Julia moaned and ran her hand up the corded muscles of her husband's arms.

"Whatever suits you is fine with me, Mr. Shelling. Just fine."

30313040R00145

Made in the USA
Charleston, SC
11 June 2014